Charlie opened the gate and said something fiercely to Hugh as he went through, which Rowan didn't catch. They all stood in a line along the fence, watching, and Hugh made
Swallow t … ame back
at a very s … ked three
times, anc … nade him
do it, alth … her time
trying to r … uptly and
Swallow … did look
splendid, …

'Wonderful!' Debbie cried. 'And he's good at jumping?'

'I'll show you!' Hugh shouted . . .

Swallow, the Star is the third title in K.M. Peyton's High Horse series about Rowan and her friends, the Hawes family.

By K.M. Peyton, and published by Corgi Books:

The High Horse series
THE SWALLOW TALE
THE SWALLOW SUMMER
SWALLOW, THE STAR

THE WILD BOY AND QUEEN MOON

Published by Corgi Yearling Books:

POOR BADGER

Swallow, the Star

K. M. PEYTON

CORGI BOOKS

SWALLOW, THE STAR
A CORGI BOOK : 0 552 529702
First publication in Great Britain

PRINTING HISTORY
Corgi edition published 1998

Set in 12/15½pt Monotype Bembo by
Phoenix Typesetting, Ilkley, West Yorkshire.

Corgi Books are published by Transworld Publishers Ltd,
61–63 Uxbridge Road, Ealing, London W5 5SA,
in Australia by Transworld Publishers (Australia) Pty. Ltd,
15-25 Helles Avenue, Moorebank, NSW 2170,
and in New Zealand by Transworld Publishers (NZ) Ltd,
3 William Pickering Drive, Albany, Auckland.

Made and printed in Great Britain by
Cox & Wyman Ltd, Reading, Berkshire.

CHAPTER ONE

Rowan got depressed sometimes, thinking she couldn't ride and never would. She was small for her twelve years, mousy in colour and quick and bright, but with an inferiority complex – especially when faced with her horsey friends, the Haweses, who had all ridden from age one. She kept her pony Swallow at the Haweses' farm, just up the road from where she lived in the village of Long Bottom. Swallow was a high-spirited and difficult pony, a great jumper but wild with it, and the Haweses could all ride him better than she could and she knew, in her heart, that they all thought she should give him up for something easier. Hugh, the fourth down of the five Haweses, coveted Swallow, although he had a very good jumping pony of his own, called Cascade. Hugh was brash and boastful, the same age as Rowan.

'I've had a very interesting letter – it concerns Hugh.'

Rowan was in the Haweses' big kitchen when Auntie Millie Mildmay, the boss of the local Pony Club, came in waving a typewritten screed. Auntie Millie was an elderly, extremely tough, ex-point-to-point rider whom everybody loved and was scared stiff of at the same time. She was crippled with old injuries, had hairs on her chin, and eyes that went straight through you and out the other side.

Mrs Hawes waved her to a seat at the large table where her children and Rowan were in the various stages of eating fried potatoes and scrambled eggs which she was lobbing out at the stove.

'Make Mrs Mildmay a cup of coffee, Lizzie,' she said.

Lizzie was Rowan's best friend, although two years older. She was a thin, quick girl with pale frizzy hair that made a halo round her head. She, too, had an inferiority complex because Hugh, who was younger, was a better rider than she was – or so she thought. He was much bolder and braver, but their older brother Charlie said having sense counted for a lot and she had more sense than

Hugh. Charlie was eighteen and the best of the lot. Rowan adored him.

'What concerns me?' Hugh asked. 'Something nice?'

'Very,' said Auntie Millie. 'But it's for your mother to say. Wait till she sits down.'

'I want something nice to happen to me,' said Shrimp, who was the youngest.

'Don't we all?' said her mother, coming to the table. 'Why is Hugh so lucky?'

She sat down next to Millie Mildmay and took the letter Millie handed her. She read it through, then read it again, while everyone politely waited to find out what it was all about. Impatiently.

Hugh said, 'Well?'

Mrs Hawes looked at Auntie Millie and grimaced.

'I thought Hugh,' Auntie Millie said. 'Unless of course you disagree with a child of yours being involved in this sort of thing.'

'What sort of thing?' Hugh shouted.

His mother looked at him thoughtfully. 'It's a film producer, looking for a boy to play a part in a film, involving some very difficult riding.'

'Hugh can't act,' Shrimp said. 'He was a terrible Mr Toad.'

'I can ride!'

'That's what they want,' Auntie Millie said. 'I think they say it's just the riding – there's already a boy playing the part, but he has to have a stand-in for the riding. That's the job that's going. They've written to several Pony Clubs to try and find someone.'

'Of course I can do it!' Hugh shouted.

'Well, I'm not against it,' his mother said. 'They should pay you for it, after all.'

'Of course. And hire of the pony. I think you supply your own pony. If you agree to it, I'll ring the producer and say I've got the man for the job.'

'If Hugh wants to, I'm quite agreeable,' his mother said.

'Of course I want to!'

'It'll make him unbearable,' Lizzie said. 'A film star! He's big-headed enough already.'

'We can all go to the first night, in Leicester Square!' Shrimp said.

'If we can fight our way in through Hugh's fans,' Charlie said solemnly.

'I'll get famous!' Hugh shouted.

'Famous for being a swollen-headed show-off!'

'He's bad enough already!'

'Do you mind?' their mother said sharply. 'Finish your disagreements outside, please, not at the table.'

Charlie said curiously, 'What do they mean by difficult riding? Underwater? Cantering backwards?'

'I'm sure I don't know,' said Auntie Millie. 'The young man will come down and see you, I dare say. The producer is a stepbrother of one of my godsons. Whatever it is, I'm sure Hugh will cope.'

Hugh grinned. His blue eyes jeered across the table at the girls. He had short blond hair and was wiry and tough and was obviously going to be rather handsome, which depressed them utterly. Lizzie and Rowan slipped out to the stables as soon as they had finished.

'Trust him to get a job like that! Why didn't they want a girl?' Lizzie moaned. Then she added crossly, 'But if they'd wanted a girl, I suppose Shrimp would've got it.'

Not only did poor Lizzie think that her younger brother rode better than she did, she also suspected that ten-year-old Shrimp did. Unlike the rest of the Haweses, Lizzie was not totally committed to The Horse.

'I suppose you want to go for a ride?' she said to Rowan. 'Not just mess about?' she added hopefully.

'Yes, I want to go for a ride.'

Rowan wasn't allowed to ride out on Swallow

alone. If there was no-one to ride with, she had to ride in the school or in the small fenced field, which was boring.

'I'll ride Jones,' Lizzie decided.

Jones was the pony everyone thought Rowan ought to buy because he was good and honest and did everything right without frightening the living daylights out of his rider. He was a dark-blue roan of nondescript breeding, but well made. Not as handsome as Swallow, of course – was any pony? (No.) Swallow put his head over the door of his loose-box and gave a low knucker of welcome when he saw the girls coming. He had been got in from the field and groomed before tea and he knew a bit of fun was now in the offing. It was April and his blanket clip was growing out, his nearly black coat gleaming with well-being, showing the slightly blueish cast which had prompted Rowan to christen him Swallow. He was just over fourteen hands, a Welsh with a dash of thoroughbred, Charlie said (although nobody knew for sure), aged about six. He had a mysterious past, having been found roaming, and although Rowan technically owned him, he had been stolen in the past and no-one had ever found out who his original owners had been. Rowan had nightmares sometimes about them turning up and claiming him.

Rowan hugged him and kissed his soft, golden brown nose as she pulled his bridle on. In the next box Cascade kicked the door and put his eager white head out to see where Hugh had got to. He wanted to go out too, but Hugh wasn't allowed to ride with Rowan and Swallow, as he would never go steadily. Charlie insisted that Swallow was only ridden steadily out on the downs, with no galloping, and only a short canter *uphill* in one or two special places. And no cantering coming home. He was very strict.

'I want you to succeed on Swallow, Rowan,' he said. 'Not get carted and frightened to death.'

Rowan was slowly getting more confident, but the pony's nature wasn't going to change.

'This sort,' Charlie said, 'they're tearaways still, even when they've gone thirty.'

The two girls saddled up and rode out into the lane. High Hawes lay near the top of the long down that enclosed the village, and they could ride out through an old oak wood above the house straight on to the fine old turf of the down. Rowan loved the spring evenings, riding through the uncurling green of the woods and smelling the fresh growth pushing out of the earth, and the damp peat turned up by the ponies' hooves. Swallow went eagerly as always. She never had to touch him with her heels and often had to remind herself not to hold on to his mouth too strongly.

'Don't fight him,' Charlie said. 'Give and take.'

Except she did the giving and he did the taking.

But dependable Jones kept a steady pace coming out through the gate on to the lovely turf. This is where Cascade always bolted off with Hugh encouraging him. Swallow curvetted and pranced to show what he wanted, but Rowan tucked him close to dear Jones and tried to make herself relax and flump in the saddle. A relaxed bottom told him no go, Charlie said. Pretend you're a big fat lady. (Auntie Millie said Charlie wasn't a brilliant teacher, more a doer.)

'I wish I could be a film star,' Lizzie said. 'Why does it have to be Hugh?'

Rowan desisted from pointing out that as they wanted a boy it was unlikely they would choose Lizzie.

'A stand-in's not a film star,' she said. 'More like a stuntman. They spend all their time hanging about waiting, I think. It might be miles away. I don't suppose we shall see anything of it.'

'It'll be fun to watch. They might have a famous film star in it, and we could talk to him, get his autograph.'

'Hugh might get discovered!'

'Like Shrimp said, he can't act. I don't suppose it'll be anything much. Shall we trot here?'

Lizzie was kind enough to ask. Hugh would have been away like the clappers by now. Rowan eased Swallow cautiously after Jones, feeling him bouncing beneath her. If he didn't get what he wanted he would buck. Rowan had learnt to sit his bucks, but didn't like them. Charlie had told her that she must be firm with him. 'But try not to make it a fight. He's bound to win if it becomes a fight.' Lizzie was understanding, and kept her eye on Swallow as she increased the pace. If he behaved, there was a lovely long canter up a grassy track that made for the brow of the hill, and a steep bank at the top acted like buffers for a grateful Rowan. At last she had learned to keep Swallow in hand as she cantered, answering to the bit, no longer in danger of bolting . . . at least she thought she had . . . but she usually felt anxious. She recalled Hugh's total confidence and courage in riding, how he laughed as he turned in the saddle to see who was keeping up with him. She knew she had a long way to go. She was determined to be good enough to master Swallow completely, and laugh too, instead of bite her lip nervously. It was all right for Lizzie – she didn't care; she just wanted to enjoy herself, no more. With her lifetime's practice, she couldn't help being good. But Lizzie had no competitive spirit. Rowan knew she had a competitive spirit, although she had done no more so far than win a potty Pony Club rosette in the Junior cross-country on Jones, who did it all for you. (In the same event Hugh had ridden Swallow and been bucked off.)

Coming to the bank, Swallow dropped his nose and came back to a walk, and they scrambled up calmly. Rowan felt a great joy swell in her as they breasted the top of the down and saw the green humpbacks of the hills beyond basking in the evening sun – it seemed far more than eighteen months since she had been a city child with only roofs for a skyline and the smell of buses in her nostrils. She could scarcely remember her before-Swallow time – whatever did she *do* in those days? Piano lessons and extra dancing . . . what a waste of time! As the wind spun in her face she looked down the way they had come and saw the golden stone and thatch of the High Hawes farmhouse nestling beneath the oak wood as if it had grown there, surrounded by its old barns and horse yards. Below, the Haweses' fields ran down into the valley where the village lay, to meet the lazy river that wound through the bottom. The ponies stood there when it was hot, under the scraggy willows, and it was miles to catch them unless they decided to gallop up at the rattle of pony nuts in a bucket. It was a magic place to Rowan and she never stopped thinking how lucky she was.

When they got home they found Hugh in the yard working on Cascade with Charlie's clippers.

'Whatever have you done!' Lizzie shrieked in horror.

Cascade's mane lay in large chunks all over the yard and his crest was now bare and shaved. Hugh was standing back regarding it critically.

'It suits him, don't you think?'

'No, it looks terrible! Poor Cascade!'

The pony turned his head, ears pricked, as Swallow and Jones came past. Rowan thought the hogging quite suited him, as he was a chunky pony, a flea-bitten grey, with a strong crest. It made him look chunkier still, like a little battle-horse.

'I like it,' she said, to be fair.

Lizzie said, 'It's only because you can't be bothered to keep his mane pulled and you hate plaiting.'

Hugh grinned. True. Cascade was in the Pony Club teams and Auntie Millie expected the ponies to be properly turned out for competitions.

They brushed the ponies off and turned them out together. Rowan had to go home to get her homework done, so she fetched her bike and whizzed down the hill into the village. She lived in rather a smart house converted from a barn, but since her father had departed to live with his secretary her mother was looking for a smaller house. It was too big for two.

'It's absolutely got – *got* – to be near High Hawes,' Rowan had stipulated.

'You could alway rent one of their loose-boxes to live in,' her mother said with a grin.

Luckily they got on well and, after the shock and strangeness of being left, they were happy enough, although short of money. Mr Watkins had been a very ambitious and impatient man, difficult to live with. He had regretted leaving London to live in the country, but Rowan and her mother loved it.

'Hugh's going to be a film star!' Rowan told her mother the exciting news. 'Pity it's him, mind you.' She thought Charlie would be a brilliant film star, with his gorgeous dark eyes, gaunt cheeks and tousled black curls. All the Haweses were fair, except Charlie. (Rowan wanted to marry Charlie later.)

'He'll like that, I should imagine. He's not a shrinking violet, is he?'

Visiting the house agents, Rowan's mother found out that there was a cottage in the village for sale, but it had once been a shop and was more or less derelict. Long Bottom consisted of only one street, meandering along the valley beside the river, and as there were only about a hundred houses in it finding one for sale was not easy.

'Your father will say it's rubbish, but it could be done up. It's got a really long garden at the back, goes down to the river, and a stable. The shop used to deliver with a horse and cart, years ago. I thought perhaps it was meant – you know – you being so pony-mad.'

'Oh, yes, I know it. It's next door to that funny old woman Mrs Brundle, who takes in injured animals. She rescued Birdie – Lizzie's pony – that's where they got her from. It's nice. I'd love to live there.'

Rowan spoke with enthusiasm, as the cottage was even nearer High Hawes than their present house. The old shop was on the corner where the lane that ran up the hill to the farm left the village street.

'Do buy it! It would be lovely. I could bring Swallow down to stay the night sometimes.'

Her own stable! She knew perfectly well Swallow would hate it, being separated from his friends, but the thought was lovely.

She got out her homework and set to.

CHAPTER TWO

'They're coming! They're coming!' Shrimp rushed into the kitchen. 'A great big car! A woman in shades and a man with a cigar – they've parked in the front yard. Charlie's talking to them.'

Joan Hawes said firmly, 'If you children are going to stay in the kitchen and gawp during this interview you're to behave yourselves. No interrupting!'

Hugh was unusually quiet, looking as if he had rather gone off the idea of being a film star.

Rowan and Lizzie and Shrimp huddled up at the end of the table and tried not to feel giggly.

Charlie came in and said, 'The film people are here.'

He stood back and ushered in two people. There

was no sign of the cigar, but the woman was wearing dark glasses, and looked very sharp and towny, and had jangling bracelets and a large file clamped to her flat bosom, and the man was rather shaggy-looking in a purple anorak and suede boots. He was quite young and had a friendly face, and eyes that roved everywhere. He came forward to shake hands with Joan Hawes.

'I'm Ron Phillips, in charge of locations, and this is Debbie Manners, our casting director. I think you've been told what our brief is?'

'Joan Hawes,' said Joan Hawes, shaking hands. 'This is my son Charlie, who is in charge of the horses here, and this is Hugh, who Mrs Mildmay thinks might fit the bill for the riding part.'

'Oh dear, he's fair,' said Debbie Manners.

'Nobody said what he needed to look like.'

'No, of course. The boy we have starring in the part is dark, but if Hugh is suitable it's easily overcome with a wig.'

Lizzie gave Rowan a great nudge of glee and Shrimp nearly fell off her chair trying not to laugh.

'He won't be seen in close-up, of course.'

'What is he required to do? Will you have a coffee, or a drink?'

Charlie pulled out seats for the visitors and Joan made coffee and Ron Phillips said what a lovely place it was and Hugh sat in silence digesting the bit about the wig.

When they were all settled Debbie told them what the film was about.

'It's a film about the life of a famous jockey, Fred Archer, who rode in the eighteen seventies and eighties. At the beginning, we have scenes from his childhood. He has to be shown being schooled by his father on a rather wild pony – then there are some hunting scenes in which he is required to give the lead over a difficult jump, and then one scene where he has to jump a racehorse over a hedge. That's all. The boy we have in the role can't ride well enough. He made out he could in the audition, but I'm afraid he was exaggerating.'

'Hugh could do that,' Joan said. 'I was thinking it was going to be something stunty, but that's just plain riding, isn't it?'

'Oh, yes. But of course he has to show that he is an outstanding rider. That's the point we're making – an outstanding rider at an early age.'

Hugh began to look more enchanted. 'Do you supply the pony, or us? And the racehorse?'

'Mrs Mildmay said you had your own pony who would do whatever was wanted.'

'Yes, I have!'

Charlie said, 'And there's a string of racehorses

just over the hill, belong to a friend, if you want a racehorse that jumps a hedge.'

Ron Phillips said to Debbie, 'That's a point. We could shoot the whole thing in one site.'

'You mean here?' she said.

'From what I've seen of it, it would be ideal. The field down the bottom there, by the stream, with those willow trees and the old village behind – it's perfect for the schooling scene. And Auntie Millie said she could lay on the hunt and find a good jump for that – and if the racehorses are to hand as well – brilliant! Everything from one base. The guv'nor will love that.'

'Yes, you could be right.'

Ron turned to Joan Hawes and said, 'We hadn't been anticipating this – that we should shoot the scenes here. But, having seen it, I think it would be great if we could. What would you feel about having the film unit here for a few days?'

'What does it entail? Total disruption?'

'Not total. Some disruption, yes. There will be a lot of vehicles and people – everyone is amazed at how many people it takes to shoot a bit of film. And we would need vehicle access into the fields. We wouldn't need to come into the house.'

Joan Hawes looked at Charlie. 'It's up to you, really. You're in charge of outside.'

Since her husband Fred, a horse dealer, had died several months ago, the two eldest Haweses, Josephine and Charlie, had taken over the running of the yard, providing for the family. Times were hard.

'I don't see it as a problem. We can move the ponies, and the fields are dry enough to take the lorries. The pony fields, that is – you can't use the hay fields until after the hay is cut.'

'No. We'd only want one field. Perhaps we could have a good look round? And the pony – perhaps see Hugh in action?'

'Yes, fine.'

They all retreated outside, the girls following, agog not to miss anything. Charlie whispered to his mother, 'They should pay us well for this. We're in luck.'

Hugh ran ahead with a head-collar and fetched Cascade out of his loose-box.

'Oh, my God, he's got no mane!' cried Debbie. 'We can't have that!'

Charlie said, 'Ponies were often hogged in the last century.'

'They might have been, but I can't see Tom wanting that. A wild pony, lots of mane and tail flying, that's what we want.' She looked round and saw Swallow's head over the door, taking in all the excitement. 'Like that,' she said.

There was complete silence among the Haweses. Rowan felt her stomach tell her she wanted to be sick.

'Is that your pony too?' Debbie asked Hugh.

'No.' Then Hugh added, 'But I ride him. He's very wild, like you want.'

Charlie said sternly, 'He's not yours.' He turned to Debbie and said, 'He belongs to Rowan here,' and indicated the shrinking Rowan.

Debbie smiled at her brightly. 'Would you lend your pony, dear?'

Rowan couldn't answer. For Hugh to show off on! To gallop wildly and jump great hedges – everything they were keeping away from to calm Swallow down. But if she said no, there wasn't another pony, not to do those things. Fable wouldn't, Jones wasn't showy enough, Birdie didn't belong to them, Snowball was too small, the Armchair too ugly, Diamond likewise. Hugh was looking at her with an expression that almost frightened her: such an intense, defiant stare from his sky-blue eyes . . . why, she found herself thinking, he could well be a film start with his strong personality and instinct for showing-off . . . how could she stand in his way at the start of a great career? She looked helplessly at Charlie.

Charlie said sweetly, 'Can we think about this one? It's not as simple as it seems.'

'Of course. But could we see the pony? Could he ride it for us?'

Charlie looked at Rowan.

'Yes,' she said chokily.

Film people tended to stampede over ordinary people, she had heard her father say once. They thought if you paid enough, people would agree to anything. All the Haweses had dropped rather quiet at the turn in the proceedings, for they all knew exactly how tricky it was.

Charlie helped Hugh saddle up and Hugh stood Swallow out in the yard in front of Debbie and Ron. It was quite obvious, in the April sunlight, that he knew he was being admired. Hugh knew how to get him to stand, as if in a show, with his legs square and his head up, rein loose. He looked boldly at the film people and the wind blew his heavy mane up over his crest and he sold himself, Swallow, the star. Rowan knew she didn't stand a chance.

'Charming!' cried Debbie. 'Delightful! Tom will just love it!'

'Can you just move around the field, show us some action?' said Ron.

Charlie opened the gate and said something

fiercely to Hugh as he went through, which Rowan didn't catch. They all stood in a line along the fence, watching, and Hugh made Swallow trot down the hill, then turned him and came back at a very strong canter, nearly a gallop. Swallow bucked three times, and Rowan was pretty sure that Hugh had made him do it, although she had no idea how. She spent all her time trying to make him not do it. He pulled up very abruptly and Swallow churned around, excited, head up. He did look splendid, there was no doubt.

'Wonderful!' Debbie cried. 'And he's good at jumping?'

'I'll show you!' Hugh shouted.

'You will not!' Charlie shouted back. And to Debbie, 'Take my word for it, he can jump anything.'

Whose side was Charlie on? Rowan had no idea. Dear Charlie saying Swallow could jump anything . . . and she too nervous to ask him even to canter . . . it was pathetic. She felt a great despair come over her, and couldn't bear to look.

'That's enough,' Charlie said to Hugh. 'Put him away.'

The film people made to depart, going through into the front yard. They all followed. As they went to get into their car, Charlie's eventer, Out of the West, stuck his head out over his door, all ears and eyes. Debbie the casting director was immediately smitten by his gorgeous head.

'Oh my word, what a beautiful beast! Can we get him in our film as well? Could he be the race-horse that jumps the hedge?'

'Hugh doesn't ride this horse,' Charlie said.

'I could,' said Hugh.

'What a looker!' said Debbie, peering in over the door. Certainly they all knew Out of the West was a looker, also that he was young, wayward and a very strong ride. He was being trained by Charlie for a rich man who thought they would all make a fortune out of him one day. Charlie thought they might, but not as soon as Mr Hicks thought. Mr Hicks had bought him for his sixteen-year-old daughter Priscilla, but had come, with great difficulty, to accept that the horse was much too much for a young girl. Charlie lived in hope that his own horse Wilfred might prove a more suitable horse for Priscilla, and was training them both together towards that end. The finances of High Hawes now depended largely on Mr Hicks.

'Well,' said Debbie, smiling, 'you seem to have everything we need here. We didn't realize it would be so good. Perhaps if we ring you tomorrow, we can talk terms and make some plans? When I've got back to our director . . . we are ready to start quite soon and it would be great if we could have a quick decision.'

She spoke in such a way that suggested she did not expect to be told no. Nobody ever told her no, Rowan thought, looking at her hard, bold face and piercing eyes. Rowan wished she was like that, bossy and tough. She knew she had lost before she started. How could she stand in Swallow's way, any more than Hugh's? He was a natural star. A little bit of her felt excited at the thought of seeing him in the cinema. She could have a video and watch him over and over again, being a star. If only it wasn't Hugh on his back . . . If she'd been good enough she could have got the job, even if she was a girl . . . had a haircut, and been filmed from the back . . . She went into a dream, seeing herself as the infant Fred Archer. She knew about Fred Archer, because she had a book at home which described his sad and dramatic life.

After the film people had departed they all went back to the house to discuss what had happened. Rowan immediately said she didn't mind Hugh riding Swallow, because she knew she couldn't stand in the way of this great bonanza for the Haweses.

Lizzie whispered, 'Liar! You *do* mind.'

'Shut up,' Rowan hissed back sharply.

Hugh said complacently, 'Charlie did give him to you, after all. You didn't buy him.'

This was so patently a twisting of the complicated route by which Rowan had come to own Swallow that the rest of the family turned on Hugh and told him to shut up. But Hugh was on a high of excitement, thinking he was going to be a film star, and only laughed.

Rowan said hurriedly, 'I wouldn't want to stop the whole thing happening. She did seem to want Swallow.'

'He's the only one suitable,' Charlie said, 'apart from Cascade.'

Josephine, the eldest Hawes, who gave Rowan most of her lessons, said quietly, 'You haven't got to, Rowan. We don't mind either way.'

'I do,' said Hugh.

'We don't care about you. It's Rowan that matters.'

'No. Honestly. It's all right.'

In spite of their consideration, she knew perfectly well that they all wanted the excitement – and the money – of the film being made.

'Well, I dare say it will only take a day or two,' Joan Hawes said. 'It's not a whole epic – only a little scene. You needn't get big ideas, Hugh.'

But everyone could see it was a good part. What had she said: the point of the scenes was to show that the boy was an outstanding rider? No wonder Hugh had such a cheesy grin on his face.

Of course they were all very excited and gabbled about it all the evening and Rowan came round to seeing that it wasn't really a great disaster, but a great honour for Swallow, and she went home eventually with her jealous feelings dissipated. It just made her all the more determined to be good enough to ride Swallow.

But when she got home she found her mother had gone off to look at the cottage-cum-shop down the road. She went out of the house to go and look for her and met Babar coming up to post a letter. Barbara Bailey was the farmer's daughter from Low Bottom Farm, who rode up at High Hawes where she had fallen for the chestnut cob known as the Armchair. All her life she had ridden her own knock-kneed, ewe-necked black weed called Diamond, and now she was suffering a guilt complex for having transferred her affections. The Haweses called her Babar the Elephant because of her shape, but she didn't mind. She talked like a yokel but was terribly clever at school, better than all of them.

She came along to the cottage with Rowan, and

Rowan told her about the excitement up at the farm, and about Swallow being the chosen pony for Hugh.

'Cor, that's rotten on yer.' Babar understood immediately.

'Well, I don't mind,' Rowan said valiantly.

'Aye, but Hugh! Anyone but Hugh, I'd say. 'E's got designs on your pony, you can see it a mile off.'

'He hasn't!'

'Yeah, 'e wants 'im to ride in the team. Cascade's good, but 'e's not as good as Swallow, anyone can see that. And Mrs Mildmay, like, she said Swallow could be a JA if 'e got trained right, 'e's got such a lep in 'im.'

'What's a JA?'

'It's the top class for show-jumpers, ponies, that is. J stands for Junior.'

'I couldn't do that!'

'No, but Hugh could.'

Whose side was Babar on? Rowan wondered wildly. Her confidence was draining away by the minute. They had reached the cottage and Rowan could see her mother inside with the estate agent.

'You goin' to buy this old place?' Babar asked.

'I don't know. It's got a stable.'

'Aye. Old Mr Markham used it for 'is 'oss to deliver with. Ages ago, that is. It were a grocer's store.'

They went in a side gate and walked through into the back garden which was a tangle of elder and nettles. There were some old sheds, and the last one was quite a decent loose-box with a half-door, a brick floor and an old wooden manger along the back, its edge polished smooth with the rubbing of generations of horses. Rowan rubbed her fingers over the silky wood. She thought suddenly she would be happy with just any old pony, living here, and no competition. Just to hack out on, and enjoy, no traumas. No trying to keep up with the Haweses. Ride with them, but not compete. The Haweses were all natural competitors, even Lizzie, who pretended she wasn't. They couldn't help it. She would always be the one trying to keep up, and she didn't see how she ever would, not against them. Was it worth trying?

'Perhaps Swallow suits Hugh better than me,' she said sadly.

'They're two of a kind – bossy, pig-headed. Doesn't mean as they're suited though.'

'Hugh could ride anything.'

'Aye, but to get one that clicks with you, just right – that's another thing. He clicks with

Cascade, you can see. But Hugh – 'e's never satisfied, always looking for the next thing, that's 'is trouble.'

'Lizzie didn't click with Birdie,' Rowan said, considering Babar's philosophy. 'She likes Fable much better.'

'That's what I mean. And yet Birdie's a much better pony.'

'Matty didn't click with Birdie either!'

Birdie was a very pretty bay mare which had been Lizzie's but, because she didn't like her, had been sold to Matty Prebble, the village's show-jumping high-flyer. But at Pony Club camp there had been an accident, Matty had been badly injured and the aggressive Mrs Prebble had sent Birdie back to High Hawes demanding her money back. As she had no evidence that the accident was Birdie's fault – in fact, the evidence was to the contrary – Charlie refused to repay her, and Birdie was now residing at High Hawes in a sort of limbo, belonging to no-one.

'Poor Birdie,' Rowan said.

'Birdie came from next door here,' Babar said. 'Mrs Brundle rescued her. Did you know that? Like she rescues everything.'

By looking through a window above the manger they could see into Mrs Brundle's back garden and, to prove the point, they could make out a large aviary housing two barn owls and several pens containing a seagull, some hedgehogs, a small badger and lots of ex-battery hens with no feathers. Grazing on the lawn was a thin donkey and an even thinner pony. Lots of cats and dogs lay out on the back terrace of the once very beautiful house, the Old Rectory, which now looked as if it, in its turn, needed rescuing.

'You'll 'ave 'er for a neighbour, come you live 'ere,' Babar said. 'She's bonkers, like. All right, but bonkers.'

Rowan tried to picture her mother being neighbourly with old Mrs Brundle, who wore a terrible old gabardine mac tied round the middle with a piece of baler twine. Mrs Bundle, she was called by the Haweses. Rowan had thought her mother was making very good progress at turning into a countrywoman, mostly helped by her friendship with Joan Hawes and getting involved with the Pony Club. Coming from Putney, she had been frightfully smart and gone to the hairdresser's every week, and the house had been like an advertisement for polish and floor-cleaners, but now dishevelment was setting in on all fronts and Rowan didn't have to keep changing her shoes outside the kitchen door, and they ate off their laps watching the television instead of at a polished table with a bottle of wine.

Rowan and Babar left the stable and went in by the back door into the kitchen, as it was open. The kitchen was ancient, still with a stone sink and a pantry and no sign of any machinery except a terrible old gas cooker. The room beyond, with the shop window, was large and light and had stairs going up out of it to the bedrooms, which all seemed to be on different levels.

'It's awfully small,' Rowan said to her mother.

Her mother had obviously changed her mind about earlier dreams of a sweet little country cottage, and was looking rather depressed.

'No bathroom,' she said glumly.

And the loo was outside, Rowan had discovered.

'But only just,' the estate agent beamed. 'It could easily be joined on, a downstairs cloakroom added.'

'It needs such a lot doing to it!'

'Oh, come, a property of character!'

'Too much character.'

The estate agent drove off and they all walked home together. Mrs Watkins said they ought to go up and visit Matty sometime.

'She's out of hospital now and very bored, I understand, poor child.'

'She could come and watch the filming,' Rowan said.

Her mother said, 'I'm glad it's Hugh they wanted and not you!'

'However could it be me?' Rowan asked in tones of deep scorn.

'I thought you were a good little rider now,' her mother said brightly.

'Well, you thought wrong.'

Her parents were hopeless. After six lessons her father had thought she could ride. He thought anyone could do it. Her mother was nearly as bad.

'I'm just a beginner. I shan't be any good for years!'

'Oh dear. Well, you haven't got to do it, you know. It's supposed to be fun, not a disaster.'

Fun! Just at that moment Rowan couldn't see it.

CHAPTER THREE

Great excitement stirred in Long Bottom at the news of a film company coming to perpetuate their sleepy valley. High Horse Equestrian Centre was suddenly on the map. Dates were fixed. Rowan groomed Swallow every day until he shone as never before. 'You'd think Hugh would do it – he's getting all the glory,' Lizzie said, but the girls knew boys never groomed or cleaned their tack unless violently coerced. Mrs Prebble called to see what was going on, and Joan Hawes invited her to bring Matty up to watch. They all loathed Mrs Prebble, but they were desperately sorry for Matty. Matty was fourteen and, away from her mother, all right. Mrs Prebble had been very ambitious for her and taken her show-jumping all over the country but, since her accident on Birdie last summer, she was stuck in a wheelchair most of the time, or lurching about on a pair of crutches.

She came out into the stable yard in her wheelchair and sat watching Rowan brushing out Swallow's thick tail.

'Where's Birdie?' she asked.

'She's in the field.'

'Doesn't anybody ride her?'

'She doesn't belong to us, does she? She's still yours. Charlie won't let us ride her.'

'Well, she's no good to me any more. Why don't you have her back?'

'I think it's money,' Rowan said. 'Your mother wants her money back and I think Charlie's spent it.'

'Oh, what good's money?' said Matty sweepingly. 'Ma's got tons. It's a shame if nobody rides her and she doesn't do anything. I'd forget about the money.'

All very well Matty saying that, Rowan thought, but Mrs Prebble had threatened to sue the Haweses over Birdie.

'I thought you didn't like Birdie,' Rowan said.

'She didn't like me,' Matty said.

Charlie had said that the Prebbles expected too much of Birdie and got her all uptight; she was only young. Remembering her conversation with Babar, Rowan thought that poor Birdie hadn't found anybody yet to click with. Like me, she thought. Clicking with Swallow wasn't really happening, however much she tried to pretend it was.

'When's this filming starting?' Matty asked.

'Tomorrow. That's why he's got to look good.'

It was the week of half-term so they were all going to watch. Joan Hawes had asked for it, not wanting Hugh to miss school, and the film company had agreed, mainly because it suited them as well. Apparently the rest of the film was already shot, and only the childhood scenes remained to be made. Tom, the director, said that, if all went according to plan, the film would be in the cinemas before the end of the year.

Rowan kissed Swallow's soft muzzle. Swallow gave her a gentle, friendly rub. If only he was as sweet when you were on his back!

'I'd like to be a film star,' Matty said. 'Wish it was me.'

Rowan felt embarrassed. Poor Matty! She was rather beautiful, with a pale skin, large violet-blue eyes and shining black hair. But she'd never be a film star now, with her damaged leg. It wasn't for ever, apparently, but walking again was going to take a long time.

Rowan said, on an impulse, 'Couldn't you ride a quiet pony – instead of the wheelchair, I mean? Just for transport. You could come up here then without your mother having to bring you.'

'I don't know. Perhaps I could. My mother keeps talking about when I will ride again.'

'I don't mean show-jumping. I mean, like a bicycle,' Rowan said.

Mrs Prebble was such a forceful mother. Thank goodness I don't have one of those, Rowan thought! They were quite a common breed in the Pony Club. Matty was an only child, and poor Mrs Prebble was now frustrated by no longer having a competitor. If Matty became able to ride again, she wouldn't get a bicycle sort of pony, but no doubt another show-jumper.

Now that the filming was imminent Hugh had gone much quieter and they all guessed he was quite nervous. He had had interviews with the director, Tom, a terse, short-tempered man whom everyone jumped to attention for, and the cameraman, who was called Ernie and seemed very laid-back. Hugh had to appear in three scenes: one in the bottom field in which he was being schooled over jumps by his father (who was quite a well-known actor), one in which he had to give a lead over a jump to his elders and betters while out hunting, and the last scene, which was set in a racing yard where he had to ride in a string of thoroughbreds at exercise and jump a hedge at the whim of his trainer. All these scenes had been discussed with Charlie and Mrs Mildmay, and Mrs Mildmay had arranged for some hunting people to come along for the hunting shot, and Charlie had arranged for his racing friend Jerry Patterson to bring six of his horses over for the day, with riders, to shoot the hedge-jumping scene. In the film story the racehorses had been young flat racers that had never jumped in their lives, and the young Fred Archer had jumped the hedge at the bidding of his master on a horse that had never been asked to jump before, which he did with consummate ease. In the film, of course, they would use a horse which knew how to jump a hedge. Nobody had quite decided which horse this was going to be, as Jerry said his horses only jumped hedges when presented at them flat out from fifty metres off, and in the film the horse was required to jump almost from a standstill, turning out of the string to do so.

'There's only one horse around here that will do that,' Charlie said. 'And that's one we can't use.'

'Out of the West.' They all knew who he meant.

They all assumed Auntie Millie would turn up

with a suitable animal on the day. That scene was to be shot last.

They hadn't counted on how the attractions of getting in on the act affected people. When Priscilla Hicks heard how Out of the West had been admired by Debbie, the casting director, she had cried out with enthusiasm, 'Oh, do let him be in the film! It would be marvellous!'

Charlie said, 'It would be crazy!'

'But you know he can do it!'

'He could if I was riding him, but I haven't got the part,' Charlie pointed out. 'Hugh's got to do it.'

'But Hugh's a brilliant rider! Everyone says so.'

'He rides ponies well. He's never ridden a horse like Out of the West.'

'But – surely? – Dad would love to have the horse in a film.'

'It's very spooky conditions for a horse, filming. The cameras and the sound boom overhead – all that sort of thing. Anything could happen.'

'Oh, do, *do* get them to use Jack!' (Out of the West was called Jack for every day.)

They all knew that Debbie the casting director still hankered after using the horse. It was true that Out of the West was spectacularly good-looking, with a natural presence. He was black, with a coat you could use as a mirror covering rippling muscle. He was shortly to take part in his first One Day Event, ridden by Charlie. Priscilla still thought she would be good enough to ride him eventually when Charlie had schooled him sufficiently, but Charlie said he would never be a girl's horse. Not Priscilla's, at least. He hadn't exactly said this to Priscilla yet. One had to be so tactful with the Hicks family, for Mr Hicks was another of the Mrs Prebble variety, an ambitious parent. Fortunately Priscilla was getting on quite well with Charlie's horse, Wilfred. She came for lessons three times a week, having recently left school. She was a rather spoilt rich girl, almost as good-looking as Out of the West, with spectacular long, curling red hair and large brown come-hither eyes which she used to good effect on the susceptible Charlie. He was much attracted to Priscilla, but disappointed to find her rather stupid.

Rowan suspected that Priscilla would be well to the fore on filming day, posing in front of the director. In that she was not mistaken, for the Hickses' car rolled into the yard shortly after the director's on the first filming morning. There was no shortage of spectators, for Mrs Prebble had brought Matty up and Rowan and Lizzie and

Shrimp were all lined up to see Hugh go through his paces. Charlie had taken on the job of horse adviser, the director having little idea of how one schooled a pony over jumps.

'The script says that Fred was more frightened of his father than the pony, which was very wild. His father ran after the pony with a whip and threw clods of earth at it to make it jump.'

Tom Ballantyne, the director, talked to Charlie in the yard while the crew drove the gear down the field to where the filming was to take place. The ponies had all been gathered up and put in the stables for the day. There seemed to be an amazing number of vehicles, with vans for dressing-rooms, make-up, costume and office as well as trucks containing the filming gear and cars full of electricians, and people with titles like grips, best boy, gaffer and runner. Catering was to arrive later in another cavalcade of kitchen, serving and dining-room vehicles.

The Haweses and their friends looked on in astonishment as all this paraphernalia came up the lane to park around the farm. Half the village trailed up behind it to see what was going on. Hugh by now had gone as white as a sheet but had been rousted out of hiding by the film people and taken to the costume and make-up vans, presumably to be turned into a lookalike of the young actor, Sam Marshall, who played the part of Fred.

Sam Marshall, the Haweses could see, bore no resemblance to Hugh at all, save that he was the same shape.

Charlie did not look too happy to hear what was required by the script.

'I hope it won't need too many takes – throwing clods of earth and all that. It's a pretty excitable pony without someone running behind it with a whip and chucking things.'

'Good,' said Tom Ballantyne. 'Exactly what we want.'

Luckily Rowan was too far away to hear this exchange. She was busy getting Swallow ready, for Charlie had said, as it was her pony, she could bring him down the field and be his handler. Everyone else had to stay out of the way. Swallow was already pop-eyed in his loose-box, excited by all the unusual traffic, and twirled round in the yard when she brought him out. Such was her lack of confidence that Rowan was now frightened he would tear out of her hands before she got him to the required place. But Charlie came over and Swallow calmed down.

They went down the field together. The

technicians had set up their gear and there was a sort of railway line with a trolley on it that ran along carrying the camera and the cameraman. One of the large willow trees had keeled over some time ago and the director seemed to think it was just the thing for Swallow to jump.

He came up to them and said, 'What we want – first, Archer senior and young Fred on the pony – we see them back view going down the field. That will be your boy. Then we have a close-up scene of the father telling young Fred to ride the pony round, put it through its paces, etc. – that will require Sam on the pony. Then – cut – the pony cantering away and jumping etc., with young Hugh on it. He'll have to do it a few times as we shall want both long shots and close-ups.'

Rowan felt quite nervous, so what on earth was Hugh feeling? He came out of the costume van with the young actor, Sam, and Rowan hardly recognized him. They both wore identical clothes, old-fashioned boys' gear, knickerbockers and stockings and Norfolk jackets, and ugly caps pulled well down, and they did look amazingly alike. Sam was said to be fourteen, but his voice hadn't broken and, close-up, he was naturally dark with large soulful eyes accentuated by make-up.

Hugh came up to get Swallow, and had the grace to blush when he came face to face with Rowan. He mumbled something and pulled the stirrups down. He rode away to meet the actor playing his father, who looked familiar to Rowan, but she didn't know who he was.

Sam came over to Rowan and stood watching.

'That your pony?'

'Yes.'

'Why didn't they give you the job, riding? It's all long shot. You're the same shape.'

'I can't ride as well as Hugh.'

'I'd have thought, if it was your pony, you'd be better.'

Rowan didn't like to say he thought wrong. She didn't know what to say after that, not knowing anything about the acting trade. It seemed to her that it involved a lot of hanging around doing nothing. But Sam, although so glamorous, seemed a patient sort of boy and stood glumly watching.

'Do you get off school for this?' Rowan asked.

'I'm at acting school. We get time off for jobs.'

'Do you like it?'

'It's all right,' he said, unenthusiastic.

It occurred to Rowan that he too might have an ambitious parent in the background, enrolling him in an acting school. It wasn't the sort of thing a child did for himself.

When he was called for his scene, talking to his father while mounted on Swallow, it was quickly apparent that he couldn't ride and that Swallow was not going to stand still for even a few minutes. Charlie had to dive in quickly to catch Swallow by the bridle and stop him tearing off.

'He's got to stand still,' Tom said tetchily.

Charlie said shortly, 'We were asked to supply a wild pony. This is a wild pony.'

'Well, for this shot he's got to stand still. You must hold him out of shot.'

Rowan had to come up and stand at his quarters to stop him swinging away from the camera. If she bent down she wouldn't be seen in the film. At the front end Charlie had to block Swallow from swinging forward and duck down when the camera rolled. Sam had to sit undismayed, listening to a harangue from his father.

This took six takes. Rowan couldn't believe the frustration of it. When they got Swallow right, a helicopter came over, drowning out the sound. A second time a tractor went up the lane. Once when Swallow stood really still, Sam fluffed his lines. Twice Swallow swung out of shot, in spite of his sweating handlers, and Rowan got trodden on painfully. When at last the take was successful, it seemed to have taken all morning.

Then they had to film the father saying his lines against the correct background which – without Swallow's involvement – took only two takes. At Tom's bidding Hugh came and mounted Swallow again and Sam disappeared back to one of the numerous vans. A props girl came down the field with a driving whip which she gave to the actor, and then proceeded to empty a bucket of clods of earth around a marked area.

Charlie and Rowan had to retreat, and left Hugh riding an already agitated Swallow round behind the cameras to 'get him hyped up'.

Charlie looked as worried as Rowan felt.

'He's hyped up enough already.'

Hugh shouted, 'If I jump the log, that'll get him tizzed up.'

'Idiot,' Charlie muttered.

It was apparent that Hugh wanted exactly what the director wanted, but for a different reason, to show off. He was rising to the part, seeing himself on the wide screen. He turned Swallow and went bombing off towards the log. Swallow plunged and bucked and tore towards the jump with his ears pricked, soaring over with nearly a metre to spare. Hugh came belting back and Swallow put in three huge bucks which made Rowan wince. And no-one had thrown any clods of earth yet or waved the whip.

'Great!' shouted Tom.

Hugh had to come and stand by his actor father while the clapper boy banged his boards together, and then set off at a great wave from the whip. The actor picked up one of the convenient clods of earth and flung it and shouted, 'You're racing, Fred, not out for a hack! *Racing!*' and Swallow, never having been subjected to such treatment in his life, went off down the field with a series of plunges and bucks that Hugh had considerable difficulty in sitting. The actor chased him furiously, waving the whip, and Hugh turned for the log.

Charlie groaned. Rowan felt herself come out in a cold sweat, thinking of herself in Hugh's place.

Swallow flew over the log, but on landing gave the biggest buck Rowan had ever seen and Hugh flew over his head with a terrific crump in the grass. Swallow turned and came up the field, bucking and kicking, stirrups and reins flying. Rowan ran towards him, horrified at the turn of events, and shouted out to him, 'Whoa, Swallow! Steady, boy, steady!'

So used to these words from his owner, Swallow did in fact slow down and when Rowan ran towards him he dropped his head and allowed himself to be caught.

Charlie, meanwhile, had run down to see what had happened to Hugh. Tom was shouting 'Cut!' and then, 'Great stuff! First rate! Get that pony back here!'

Hugh, however, seemed to be a long time getting up.

'God almighty, don't say he's hurt himself!' Tom said angrily.

He waited, tight-lipped, as Hugh came limping back with Charlie. Hugh was pale, but not noticeably damaged.

'OK?' barked Tom.

Hugh nodded.

'We'll do that again, but don't fall off this time.'

Rowan could see quite plainly that all the stuffing, along with the arrogance, had been knocked out of Hugh, and that Tom had no idea, absolutely no idea, of what the situation was. He saw only his film. He said to his PA girl, 'You got the boy insured, I take it?' and she nodded and said, 'Yes, of course.'

Charlie said, 'Give him ten minutes. He took a hard fall.' He spoke with such authority that Tom gave him a hard look, but did not demur.

'We'll shoot close-up on Stan.'

Stan was Fred's father, who then went through his shouting and swearing with the camera close to his face. Hugh sat on the grass, silently, and Charlie stayed with him, while Rowan led Swallow around, letting him snatch at the grass. He was sweating and nervous, but her presence reassured him. Rowan was thinking, even if Hugh was now regretting his role, he had no option but to go on with it. Perhaps he was wishing he had broken his leg?

But Hugh was made of stern Hawes stuff and when the close-up filming was finished he remounted Swallow without a word and turned him away sharply for a repeat performance.

This time he had to canter some circles, with the earth clods flying, which went without a hitch.

'It's jumping that gets that little beggar going,' Charlie said to Rowan. 'He adores it, you can see. He's got enormous talent.'

He regretted his words, for he saw Rowan's thoughts plainly registered in her abject eyes: if only I could ride him well enough to do him justice! Rowan didn't say anything, actually thinking she would never be able to ride him at all after this.

'Now jump the log again!'

This time the jump was filmed in close-up.

'It doesn't matter if you fall off this time!' Tom shouted, as if to comfort. 'We just want you going over.'

Once again, Swallow went over with about a metre to spare, and the camera looked up, from behind, so that Hugh's face wouldn't show. Rowan could see that it was a spectacular shot, all swirling tail and flying hooves. Swallow bucked again on landing but Hugh stayed on.

'Cut!'

Tom was transparently pleased. Rowan could see that directing was a very fraught business, getting it right when there were so many things to go wrong, from passing car noises to death of actor, and began to appreciate why the man got so uptight.

He even came up to Hugh and said, 'Well done! How are you feeling?'

'OK.'

But Rowan rather thought he looked terrible as she took Swallow's bridle to lead him back to the stable.

'We shoot the jump with the hunting men at three o'clock. You report to the costume van at two and come up with the actors. Meanwhile you can go and get your lunch in the canteen. You too,' he added to Charlie and Rowan.

Charlie said to Hugh, 'You might do better to come back home for an hour.'

Hugh shook his head. 'I'm OK.'

Rowan sensed that he was humiliated by having fallen off, and didn't want to meet Lizzie and Shrimp and all the hangers-on in the yard. She felt a small pang of sympathy for him, surprisingly.

Auntie Millie had some strong words when she met them at the gate.

'If I'd known how that madman was going to treat that boy and the pony, I'd never have put them forward for it! Ridiculous! He's no sense at all!'

'No horse sense,' Charlie agreed.

Rowan put Swallow in his box and untacked him and gave him a hay-net. Charlie didn't want to eat in the canteen and nor did she – they went into the kitchen where her mother had helped Joan Hawes lay out a tableful of ham and Scotch eggs and salad.

'Where's Hugh?' his mother asked.

Charlie explained.

'I hope he's not knocked himself silly.'

'He's silly enough already,' Shrimp said. 'He *fell off*, Mum, right in front of the camera!'

Charlie said, 'You wouldn't have sat that buck either.'

'So what happens next?' Joan asked.

'He's only got to jump a fairly easy jump,' Auntie Millie said placatingly. 'It's that bit of fence in the corner of the Sandpile field. He can ride up there when he's ready. Mr Sedgefield and his son are going to bring their horses up. They always refuse, so when they've tried and refused, the idea is that Hugh nips in and jumps it in front of them and gallops away. That seems to be what that madman wants. Really, if I'd known how stupid he is about horses I wouldn't have offered to help.'

'I think he might have got some good film, all the same,' Charlie said.

Rowan supposed Swallow would look pretty magnificent on the screen, but how would he behave when she came to ride him again?

In the lunch hour they discovered that Priscilla had been beguiling the film director and Debbie, the casting girl, with eulogies of how well Out of the West would jump the hedge in the scene that was to be shot the next day. They also discovered that the local press had arrived and were taking photos of all and sundry. Priscilla led Out of the West out of his box and told them he was going to be the star the following day, and they took a photo of him with Priscilla smirking at his head. Charlie shook his head in despair. Rowan, furious, fetched

Swallow out and got his photograph taken as well, and then Hugh came up from the canteen – 'Jolly good – roast *turkey* and roast potatoes, sprouts, Yorkshire pudding, gravy, apple-pie and custard' – 'You're a fat pig already!' Shrimp shouted. 'Swallow will collapse!' Hugh now wore a smarter outfit with a white stock and breeches and boots, as befitted a boy going hunting in 1868. He was already mounting, to get his photo taken as well.

'Everyone's gone mad round here,' Charlie decided.

They all had to decamp up the lane to the field Auntie Millie had chosen for the hunt jump, and the same hanging about then ensued as the camera was set up and shots discussed. The horses that always refused arrived in their lorry and their riders were kitted out in ancient hunting gear, and mounted and sent down the field with Hugh and Swallow.

Everyone lined the fence to see the fun, Rowan once more with a sinking heart and Charlie distinctly worried. Hugh was cantering Swallow in circles to get him warmed up, but it was hardly necessary.

When they started the first take, one of the refusing horses actually ruined everything by jumping the fence. His rider was so amazed he fell off and the horse galloped off and was quite a long time getting caught. Swallow, having got the idea, started bucking again before he was even asked to move. Tom was shouting angrily.

'Take two hundred and sixty-one!' The clapper man leapt back and the three horses came hurtling up the field again. This time the first one refused and the second one crashed into its backside. Hugh was supposed to pull round to jump but there was no room and Swallow skidded into the ditch at the side of the fence and Hugh landed up his neck, and all but in the thorny hedge. Pushing himself back into the saddle he shouted angrily, 'The jump isn't wide enough!'

'You're supposed to be a brilliant rider, for heaven's sake!' Tom shouted back. 'That's the whole point of it. Find room!'

'That man is seriously brainless,' Auntie Millie snapped.

She started to climb the fence to stride into battle but before she could do so the horses went into action again. This time, as the two hunters jolted to a standstill, Hugh pulled out wide and charged the hedge instead of the rails that were set in them.

Rowan heard Charlie's gasp of alarm.

Auntie Millie shouted out, 'You stupid boy!'

Swallow took off miles back and made a stupendous leap at the huge obstacle. He crashed through the top, sending twigs and leaves flying, and landed well out into the next field. Although he pecked and nearly went down Hugh sat him like a limpet, gathered him together and galloped away, no doubt feeling hugely smug and pleased with himself.

Tom was conferring with the cameraman, frowning – was he ever pleased? The sound man was complaining about someone shouting 'You stupid boy!' in the middle of the action. It would have to be done again.

'I don't believe this!' Auntie Millie snorted. 'Is this really how films are made?'

Apparently the seriously brainless Tom managed to convince her that it was, and when Hugh came back grinning all over his face he discovered that his mean feat of riding was all in vain. It had to be done again. But he didn't seem to mind.

'How he is enjoying showing off!' Shrimp groaned.

Swallow was dancing on his toes, unable to stand still, and Hugh had to ride him around to calm him down. This time the two refusers were told to try and keep to one side so that Hugh would have room to pass them. They set off one after another, but after the first horse refused the second one swung out to avoid him right across Swallow's take-off, and there was an almighty pile-up in the ditch. The horse and Swallow both went down in a great flailing of hooves.

'This is ridiculous!' Charlie decided.

After a long argument with the director it was decided, mostly by Auntie Millie, that Charlie should ride the second refusing horse as he was a strong enough rider to stop it veering off in the undesired direction. Its owner was only too pleased to agree, and swapped his clothes with Charlie out in the field to save time. 'Else we'll be here all night. The light's beginning to go already,' Tom complained.

Swallow had a great gouge of skin out of his near hindleg which was bleeding, but not badly, and the horse Charlie was to ride now had a marked aversion to going anywhere near the fence, not surprisingly. Charlie rode him around for a bit to calm him down and Auntie Millie came stalking back from the fray saying, 'Damned thing will probably jump with Charlie on its back. It always refuses because that idiot can't ride.'

It did seem to Rowan that a certain discipline seemed to descend on the operation now that Charlie had taken over and in the two subsequent takes Swallow was given just the right gap to nip through. Each time he cleared the fence perfectly. Tom was satisfied. Charlie said to Auntie Millie it was a nice horse and would jump perfectly well if given a chance, but exchanged commiserations with its owner when he went to get his own clothes back. Hugh gave Swallow back to Rowan, smirking at the congratulations, and the party started to dribble back down the hill to the farm.

'What a circus!' Auntie Millie boomed, but Tom was now all sweetness and light, having got his day's work in the can.

He was now ready to discuss the next day's jumping of the hedge. Everyone else departed but he stayed, wandering down the field with Charlie to find a suitable spot, discussing the various options. The girls turned the ponies out in their field, and Swallow galloped away, bucking and kicking with delight after his exciting day.

Rowan stood watching him go.

Shrimp said, 'He's a fantastic jumper. I wish he was mine.'

'Don't be stupid. You'd get carted,' Lizzie said derisively.

They went in for their supper and Rowan got her bicycle out to whizz home. She felt very low.

It was almost dark and the ponies were shapes in

the dusk, grazing on their favourite patch at the bottom by the river. Rowan stopped at the gate to watch them, too stirred up to go home immediately. Over the bridge she could see the back garden of the old shop she had examined the night before and the horseless stable with the elder tree growing against it. The vision of her own perfect pony who never gave her a moment's fright, looking out over the top door, came back to her with a painful twist of longing. She leaned over the gate, close to tears of frustration.

Swallow, Fable, Jones, Birdie, Snowball, the Armchair, Pinkie and her shadow Bonzo, the skewbald yearling of Shrimp's, cropped contentedly. The evening smell of the river was familiar and soothing. Rowan could see the yellow flowers of the marsh marigolds like stars scattered in the water and the green weed streaming on the current. It was a trout river – perhaps she should have taken up fishing, so restful . . .

As she lingered, one of the ponies lifted its head and looked across at her. It was a bright bay, built like a small thoroughbred, very elegant, with black points and a fine black mane and tail, two white stockings behind and a narrow white blaze.

'Birdie!'

Rowan called to her, but the pony tossed her mane and walked slowly away after the others. A mist was creeping up the valley, and in a moment they had all disappeared.

CHAPTER FOUR

When Rowan went up to High Hawes the next morning, Lizzie said to her, 'You'll never guess – Priscilla has got herself into the film! She's going to ride Wilfred in the string of race-horses. She fluttered her eyelashes at Tom and he agreed.'

'But she's a girl. They never had girls then.'

'No, but she's going to be dressed like a lad and Tom says it'll be all right if she stays at the back. She's so pushy! They're going to use Out of the West too, in spite of Charlie's not wanting to. Hugh wants to, of course.'

Rowan thought it might be quite a good idea to keep out of the way. It sounded as if it would be far more fraught than the day before. While she was thinking this, Josephine, the eldest of the Haweses, came into the kitchen, saw Rowan in her jodhpurs and said, 'Oh, good, you've come for your lesson. I thought you were off gawping with the others.'

'Well, I was going to, but I'd rather have my lesson.'

'If it's anything like yesterday, you can do both. It takes them hours to get going. We'll have finished by then.'

Rowan got on well with Josephine who, at twenty, seemed rather remote from the rest of the family. She was quiet, and did not join in the bickering. She had qualified to teach, but didn't care for it very much save one to one, which she enjoyed. She helped Charlie school Out of the West and Wilfred and went out teaching quite a bit, to people who had their own horses at home. She still didn't have a horse of her own, and Charlie was losing Wilfred to Priscilla. They both said it was a waste of money when you could ride other people's. But Rowan knew the Haweses were short of money since Mr Hawes died.

'Who shall I ride?'

Josephine looked surprised. 'Swallow?' Then she laughed. 'Or have you gone off him after his rodeo displays yesterday?'

Rowan dared not admit it. Hugh hadn't done him any good.

Josephine put a friendly hand on Rowan's shoulder.

'We'll be very quiet, bring him back to square one.'

Rowan was relieved. Josephine was sympathetic, and knew about her lack of confidence. Rowan didn't mind her knowing but she minded the others knowing.

The others had got the ponies in and Rowan had only got to brush Swallow over and tack up. She had her lesson in the manège where, whatever else, Swallow couldn't bolt. The film people hadn't yet arrived.

Rowan led Swallow out to the school and Josephine shut the gate behind her. She mounted and immediately Swallow stiffened beneath her, and snatched at his bit, tearing the reins out of her hands. Then he pranced backwards into the fence, cracking the top bar, and immediately made to leap off but Josephine caught his bridle and restrained him. Rowan felt as if she were sitting on a keg of dynamite. All her worst fears were immediately realized.

Josephine kept hold of the bridle and said to

Rowan, 'Get him to walk on. Use your legs. Gently.'

Rowan couldn't believe that she had to be led, like a four-year-old. She bit her lip to stop the tears of despair blurring her eyeballs. She inched out her reins. Swallow walked out, switching his tail, his neck bent like a German show-jumper. He seemed to Rowan to be quivering with pure mischief like a naughty child.

'Relax, Rowan. Give him some rein.'

Josephine let go, but stayed walking close to Swallow's head. Rowan sensed that Swallow respected Josephine's authority, for he too relaxed and after a couple of circuits of the school Josephine dropped to her place in the middle. Swallow walked on, switching his tail.

'Get him really settled. Walk him in figure of eights. He's got to forget he's a film star.'

It was boring, but better than being bucked off.

Josephine said, 'I don't know what his past history is, but I think he probably belonged to a nut-case like Hugh, who just galloped and jumped.'

'Charlie said he adores jumping. He was great yesterday.'

'He's very bold, no doubt about it.'

But lots of doubt about his being a suitable pony for Rowan Watkins.

After half an hour, having done serpentines and circles and changes of rein, Josephine decided they could risk a slow, steady trot. Rowan did two circuits of the school and was just starting her third when Swallow snatched at the reins, put his head down and broke into a sort of bucking canter. His head seemed to disappear altogether. Rowan sat back and tried to haul in her reins, having had a fair amount of practice, but – remembering yesterday's bucks (even *Hugh* had come off) – felt very frightened. But Josephine, springing up like a gazelle, was at his head before he had gone halfway down the school.

'You *bad* boy!' Then, severely, 'Walk on. Wa-a-a-lk on.'

Rowan was being led again.

They walked for the rest of the hour, Josephine tactfully retreating as before. But she did not ask for another trot. When they finished and Rowan thankfully slid off, Josephine grimaced and said, 'Not good. I'm sorry. That filming has gone to his head.'

Rowan burst out, 'I shall never be good enough for him! Babar said that Mrs Mildmay said—' She hiccuped with tears again – 'He's a JA or something, and Charlie – Charlie said – he—' What had Charlie said? She couldn't remember now, only that Swallow adored jumping. She was keeping Swallow from his true role in life, walking him in endless circles because she was too feeble to do anything else.

'Come on,' Josephine said. 'It's not just you, Rowan. Calm down. It's something we've got to work through. It'll take time and nobody's in a hurry. Let's put him away and you can have half an hour with one of the others. Do a bit of jumping. Which one do you want? You choose.'

'Birdie,' Rowan said.

She never knew why she said it. The name just slipped out.

Josephine gave her a somewhat shocked look and said, 'She hasn't been ridden lately. I'm not sure if it's wise.'

'She couldn't be worse than Swallow!'

'True.' And then, 'Well, why not?'

They had the place to themselves. Birdie was snoozing in her box. Rowan ran to fetch her saddle and bridle out of the tack-room, leaving Josephine frowning over the turn of events. She thought Rowan needed humouring, needed to prove herself. Riding Jones or Fable or the Armchair wasn't going to prove anything, because they were all darlings, but if she rode Birdie successfully it would cheer her up no end. Josephine, like all the Haweses, was not averse to taking a chance. Nothing ventured, nothing won.

Birdie felt completely different from Swallow; sort of slippery, Rowan thought. She felt much higher off the ground, and the pony's shoulders were much narrower and she was more delicate. The reins felt light and soft from her mouth. Rowan couldn't believe that she'd had the nerve to ask for Birdie – what had come over her? But somehow she didn't feel frightened of her like she did of Swallow. Although Birdie did not go very smoothly, but curvetted and danced about, Rowan felt quite happy. She felt that Birdie was pleased to be ridden again, and her prancings were of delight.

Josephine was very careful, watching Birdie like a hawk and assessing just how much she could ask of her without getting her tizzed up. They did trotting poles, and Josephine taught Rowan how to extend Birdie on the long sides of the school and shorten her up at the ends, which she did beautifully. Rowan had never been able to do this with Swallow. Birdie's long stride was very comfortable, and it was easy to feel the difference, shortening and lengthening. Then Josephine put a cavalletti at the end of the poles and Birdie popped over it.

Twice more and she tried to break into a canter, but at Josephine's command Rowan was able to steady her back into a trot. When she had trotted over them twice more, slowly, Josephine told Rowan to pull up.

'That was very good. We'll finish there. She's been so good!'

If Josephine was relieved, Rowan was even more so. As she slid to the ground, she was filled with the true exhilaration of success. It was only a potty success but, after Swallow, Rowan was thrilled.

'You *can* do it,' Josephine told her. 'You can ride her in a lesson again, if you want. She went very well for you.'

Rowan remembered what Babar had said about 'clicking' with a pony and wondered if, perhaps, Birdie had liked her. Perhaps Birdie lacked confidence, like she did, and felt a kindred spirit. Lizzie had never liked Birdie, and nor had Matty. But she didn't dare say this to Josephine. Josephine, like Charlie, could ride anything and looked marvellous on Out of the West and on Wilfred, with her long legs and deep, elegant seat. She schooled the two thoroughbreds in their dressage.

After the lesson Josephine went to tack up Wilfred. Rowan watched her. She longed to be able to ride like Josephine – more than being able to ride like Hugh. Even she, a beginner, could see the finesse of Josephine's riding. Charlie said anyone could bash across country on the right horse, but riding a horse in the school, doing perfect circles at a slow canter, changing legs so smoothly on to the other rein, was real riding. Rowan sensibly thought you wanted a bit of both – but, oh, how she wanted to succeed!

Josephine, as if she guessed what she was thinking, laughed and said, 'Why are you so ambitious, Rowan? It should be fun, you know. You mustn't get upset.'

'I want to ride like you. And Charlie.'

Josephine pulled up Wilfred's girth. Then she said, 'You won't learn on Swallow, you know. You're making it very hard for yourself.'

'Not ever?'

'Perhaps. But on such a strong pony you will learn bad habits.'

'Even if we go very slowly?'

'You can't change a pony's nature, Rowan. It's like people. Hugh is quite different from you. Training doesn't make you alike, does it? You will always be what God made you in the first place. Training can only improve what is already there. It can't turn a timid horse into a great cross-country winner, or a really stupid clumsy horse into a dressage champion. Swallow is a natural, born jumper, and very headstrong. He's not *able* to teach a girl like you how to ride.'

Rowan digested this information sadly. It was what she knew, in her heart, but couldn't bring herself to admit.

Josephine said, 'I'm being honest with you, because I want you to succeed. Because you want it so much yourself. If you just want to be tough and career about like Hugh, fine. You will learn to handle Swallow, if you're brave enough, but you won't be successful, because there will be no groundwork underneath. Hugh, for all he's so crazy now, learned the basics of riding on a dear little pony called Pommie who was as good as gold. Pommie looked after him like an angel. We all learned on Pommie, even Charlie.'

Rowan was silent. There was nothing to be said, although Josephine's words hurt like a physical pain. Josephine knew they did, but she thought Rowan had to know Charlie had been an idiot to give her Swallow in the first place, in her opinion.

'Come on, Rowan, it's not the end of the world! These things have a way of working themselves out. We'll think of something, between us.'

Rowan watched her ride away into the school on Wilfred. Wilfred had been bought out of the same bad riding school as Swallow and had looked like a scarecrow when Charlie had brought him home. They had all laughed. But now he had filled out and looked like the well-made thoroughbred he was. Charlie had seen what lay underneath the skin and bones. He had a very amenable nature and learned quickly and had turned out to be just the horse for the not-brilliant (but thought she was) Priscilla.

Priscilla finding Wilfred was a success. They clicked. Rowan and Swallow was not a success story, and Rowan knew it.

Before she could get too deep into the waters of despair, Rowan was distracted by the arrival of the Haweses' Land-Rover. Joan Hawes was back from a shopping expedition with Shrimp. Before the car had come to a proper halt Shrimp was leaping out, shouting at Rowan, 'Look, Rowan! Have you seen the newspapers! Look! Look!'

She came running over with a sheaf of newspapers in her hand.

'We bought lots, one for everybody! Look!'

Rowan looked and saw a magnificent shot of Swallow staring at the camera with his ears pricked up and his mane blowing in the wind. Hugh sat on his back, glowering in his flat cap and old-fashioned clothes.

The picture was captioned, 'Local Boy Helps Out Film Makers'.

Underneath there was a smaller picture of Swallow jumping the log with about a metre to spare.

'Local rider, Hugh Hawes, of High Hawes Farm, Long Bottom, stood in for young star Sam Marshall when filming took place in the village recently. Chosen for his riding skill, twelve-year-old Hugh successfully jumped his pony Swallow in several scenes from the early life of the famous jockey Fred Archer. The film is being made by . . .'

Rowan didn't bother to read any more, gazing with glowing eyes at Swallow's undeniable beauty.

'*His* pony, it says!'

'What a cheek!' Shrimp shouted. 'We'll tell him what a liar he is! Where are they all? We must show them!'

'They're all over at Jerry Patterson's racing yard,' Joan Hawes said. 'There's been a change of plan. They're going to film over there. They're sending the horse-box for Jack and Wilfred. You two can go over in the horse-box when it comes, save me ferrying you.'

Such was the excitement, Rowan's misery was

forgotten. Shrimp had bought her a copy of the newspaper for her own – perhaps they could write and get a glossy copy of the original picture? It was such a beautiful photograph.

Charlie arrived shortly, driving Jerry's horse-box, and was made to enthuse over the newspapers.

'Lucky they didn't get him falling off. It was far more dramatic,' he said unsympathetically. 'Good photo though.'

Josephine brought Wilfred in from the school and boxed him up, and Charlie fetched Out of the West. Soon they were on their way round to the next valley where the racehorses lived, several miles by road but quite quick by pony over the top of the down.

'We'll see what drama we have in store today,' Charlie said gloomily. 'I fear the worst.'

'Have you chosen the right bit of hedge?' Shrimp enquired.

'Yes. The lowest bit I could find.'

All the chaos of the day before was now being re-enacted around Jerry Patterson's yard. He was watching, bemused, as Tom ordered his string of recehorses about. A man with bushy whiskers in a black suit and a high silk topper, and another man dressed in the same fashion with a flower in his buttonhole, were chatting together in the middle of the yard while Jerry's 'lads' were being ordered to let down their stirrups and sit with their legs pushed forward and their toes down and turned out.

'This is supposed to be the eighteen sixties. That's how they rode then, none of your crouching stuff.'

They rode round, practising and larking about, while Charlie tacked up Out of the West. Priscilla came forward to take Wilfred, dressed in breeches and boots and a tweed jacket, with all her gorgeous hair pushed up into one of the ugly flat caps. She looked terrible. Rowan hoped Tom might tell her so and get Charlie to swap with her, but nothing happened and she mounted and joined the back of the string, trying to sit in the way Tom wanted.

Knowing what to expect, and not having Swallow to dote on this time, Rowan found the filming rather boring.

'It's all waiting!' Lizzie complained.

Jerry's racehorses, who had mostly been out at grass on their summer holidays, stood dozing but Out of the West, fit and hard, got progressively more fidgety while Tom messed about with his cameraman. In the end, when he was asked to jump the hedge by Hugh, he refused.

Charlie came forward crossly and said what did

they expect? He got on and schooled Out of the West for ten minutes in the field, then jumped backwards and forwards over the hedge four times. Then he slid off and said, 'Film it now, while he's expecting it.'

He legged Hugh back on and Hugh joined the string on the now fizzing Out of the West. They walked down the hedgeside and Hugh pulled him out of the string, circled him and jumped the hedge. He pulled up on the far side, and then jumped back as instructed. Then he had to do it again. All went well.

Then Tom had to take some close-ups of Sam Marshall sitting on Out of the West, listening to his instructions from the trainer, which Charlie said they should have done first, for now the big horse was excited by his jumping and wouldn't stand still. It took Charlie and Jerry between them to manhandle him into position, bending down out of shot when the cameras rolled.

Hugh had no more to do, and got changed into his own clothes, and then all the excitement was over.

It seemed a terrible anti-climax.

Charlie and Priscilla rode away over the down for home and the rest of them were given a lift back by one of the technicians. Only the fantastic photos of Swallow remained to remind them what had happened.

As Hugh and the others enthused over them, Rowan felt the cold web of despair wrap her again – *her* pony, yet not really hers at all, and never would be, if Josephine was right. Lizzie was taunting Hugh: 'It says "on his pony" – I bet you told them that – I bet you told them Swallow was yours!'

'I never!' Then he added, 'I wish he was!'

'Poor Swallow, if he belonged to you!' Shrimp shouted.

'Why don't you all go for a ride and get out of my kitchen?' Joan Hawes appealed.

They scattered out into the yard to fetch saddles and bridles. Rowan knew she couldn't ride Swallow if Hugh was coming. She had an overwhelming urge to tack up Birdie, but knew the others would think she had gone potty. While she stood dithering in the tack-room, Lizzie said, 'I'm riding Fable, so you can take Jones,' so that decided it.

Jones was a really good pony, but Rowan had never felt any proprietary interest in him, mainly because a girl in the Pony Club called Roma Glade came for lessons on him and was going to buy him. The snag was she had been going to buy him for almost a year but somehow the money had never been forthcoming. If Josephine meant what she said, Rowan supposed she would now be having lessons on him instead of on Swallow. She could not bring herself to dwell on what Josephine had said. It was like a bad dream. She wasn't even going to tell Lizzie. It hurt too much.

When they got back she went home for lunch on her bicycle. Her mother was rather quiet but Rowan supposed she was thinking about moving house and getting a divorce which preoccupied her quite a lot these days, so she tried to be helpful and said nothing about her own woes, which – although it didn't feel like it – were probably not much compared to her mother's. She told her mother about the beautiful photos of Swallow in the local paper.

Her mother said, 'Oh yes, Joan rang up and told me about them.'

She then gave Rowan a rather odd look and said, 'Joan wanted me to tell you—' She hesitated.

'Tell me what?'

'While you were out riding a man rang up. He'd seen the photos and said—' Her voice failed her again.

'Said what?'

'He said the pony belongs to him. He recognized it. It was stolen out of his yard a year ago, when he was abroad. He's only been back a couple of months and saw the photo in the paper today. He's coming over tomorrow morning.'

CHAPTER FIVE

Rowan knew what it felt like, because it had happened before. She had rescued Swallow after he had been found wandering and abandoned, and a man had claimed him dishonestly and taken him away and sold him in a market. The same dismay she remembered so clearly overwhelmed her again. Her mother commiserated sincerely, knowing that her love for Swallow and her new pony life had helped enormously in deflecting Rowan's grief from the family break-up. Now everything seemed to have fallen to pieces again.

Charlie said, 'It's not cut and dried. Swallow has been sold twice since this man lost him. He can't expect just to come in and take him away.'

'What did he sound like? Nice?' Rowan asked timidly.

Joan Hawes had taken the call. They were having a family conference the following morning.

'Cheerful. Confident. Pleasant enough. He said he'd gone abroad and left the pony with friends. The friends had then been in a car accident and had to stay in hospital and it was disaster all round, and Swallow going missing was the least of their worries apparently. It's his son's pony. Competition pony, he said.'

Rowan's worst fears were realized. A cocky boy like Hugh, no doubt, with heavy hands and big feet, all out to win. Not a sweet girl with a loving heart.

'What's his name?'

'Bill Trugg, he said.'

The Hawes family, even Hugh, were all sombre at the news. Nobody wanted to lose Swallow, for all his faults. Rowan was sure that Hugh had been hoping he would get him, after she had failed to cope with him, and have him to compete on.

Shrimp said sadly, 'He'd never have known if Swallow's photo hadn't been in the newspaper.'

And they had been so proud!

Everyone was on edge, waiting for Mr Trugg to arrive. It was a cool day, threatening rain, which fitted in with the general mood, and the ponies, let out, had all rolled in the mud. But Swallow had been kept in and groomed, to show how beautifully he was kept. His coat already shone like an advertisement for polished furniture; he was well-rounded but fit, the picture of a perfect pony.

At half-past eleven a smart BMW pulled into the yard.

'He's not short of a bob or two, at least,' Charlie commented.

Rowan was shivering and felt sick. She quickly saw that her worst fears were realized, for Mr Trugg – 'The name's Billy' – was a big brash man, the sort that exhorted his child from the ringside, and son Tom was a well-built boy of her own age, with a neck as wide as his face, a bristly head and hard, pale blue eyes behind thick glasses. Rowan took an instant dislike to them both.

'Tom Trugg,' Lizzie whispered. 'More like Tom Thug.'

'Billy Brag,' Shrimp whispered and they got the giggles. 'Billy Brag and Tom Thug.'

Rowan didn't feel like giggling.

They all went over to Swallow's box and Charlie led him out and the Truggs exclaimed with satisfaction.

'That's our boy! That's our little beaut!'

Tom Thug did show a slight enthusiasm, and patted Swallow on the neck.

'Hi, Hottie,' he said.

'Hottie?'

'His name is Hotspur.'

Even Rowan had to admit that it was a good name for him. Even that it was probably better than Swallow. She could see how it was all going to happen, and was convinced already that the pony was lost.

Charlie was telling Billy Brag that he had paid good money for Swallow, and that his present owner was Rowan. He put a hand on Rowan's shoulder and propelled her in front of their cheerful visitor. Rowan glowered.

'It's a long story. Perhaps we'd better go indoors and I'll explain what's happened.'

Nobody knew what the legal position was. Swallow had passed through several hands since the Truggs had lost him.

'We don't want to get a load of lawyers involved, surely?' Billy Brag said. 'Their bill would be ten times what the pony's worth.'

'Two families went to court about the same situation recently,' Joan Hawes remarked. 'It was reported in the paper. But at the last minute they settled and the original owners let the current owners keep the pony.'

'Well, we want this pony back, don't we, Tom?'

'Yes,' said Tom bluntly.

'He's a winner, you see. And Tom's not out of his class yet.'

'He's fairly big for him, I would have thought,' Charlie said equably.

'Getting on that way. But we've a whole summer of competing ahead of us.'

'We can't just give him to you,' Charlie said. 'You must see that. We can't afford to lose the price of him.'

'I'll pay you what you paid for him, or whatever it was he fetched on the market. That's fair enough. You won't be out of pocket, and I'll be happy to pay a reasonable sum to have him back.'

Charlie was silent. Even Rowan could see that it was an amicable, even generous, offer.

Joan Hawes, seeing the dismayed faces round the table, said, 'Perhaps, when Tom has grown out of him, there might be a chance for us to have him back?'

'Possibly, but he won't be cheap, I can promise you. Not after Tom here has got him back on the circuit. I take it you haven't been competing on him?'

'Only in the Pony Club.'

'And Hugh fell off,' Shrimp said.

Hugh kicked her under the table and she screamed.

Mr Trugg laughed and said, 'He's not an easy beggar, is he?'

Charlie, seeing Rowan's face, made a despairing try: 'We really would like to keep him if we could.'

'No way,' said the man. His expression changed and it was plain that he was no man to have for an enemy. 'I've made you a very fair offer.'

It was indisputable. He had.

'You can go to law if you want, but I'll fight you all the way.'

'Well, no, none of us want that sort of hassle.' Charlie shrugged. 'I agree you're being fair. It's just – you know – kids get to love a pony—'

He looked embarrassed and Rowan felt she had to jump in and help.

'It's all right, honestly. You know I can't ride him properly.

'It isn't all right!' Hugh hissed at her.

'Hugh!' his mother snapped.

Through all this exchange Tom Thug sat stolidly, without emotion. There was no way, Rowan thought, he had ever loved Swallow, save perhaps as a money-maker. But perhaps Swallow didn't want love. He had certainly made no bones about removing her painfully from the saddle if it suited him. Perhaps she was just a stupid sentimental twit. But Charlie had cried when he had had to sell Fedora. Love? No, frustration probably. She would be well off without Swallow, considering she only ever had trouble with him. She boldly smiled. Charlie, surprised, said, 'All for the best.'

'You're happy, kid?'

Rowan forced a sickly smile.

'Good on yer!' Billy clapped her on the shoulder so that she nearly fell over, and pulled out his cheque-book.

'What's your price?'

So the deed was done. The Haweses all watched in silence as Charlie took the cheque, and then went out with father and son to make the travelling arrangements. The Truggs only lived ten miles away.

'Oh, poor Rowan!' Lizzie wailed.

Hugh was sulking and Shrimp casting round for alternative rides for Rowan. 'You can have Jones! He's lovely. Or Diamond – Babar doesn't ride him any more. Or Bonzo when he's old enough!'

'I'm sure Charlie will find you something suitable,' Joan Hawes said. 'The money is yours, after all, because he did give Swallow to you.'

They were all extra nice to her and Rowan had to show that her heart wasn't broken, although she was quite sure it was. She turned her mind resolutely away from Swallow, and tried to make it concentrate on a lovely pony that stopped when she asked, cantered like a dream over the downs without pulling her arms out and came to the gate with a welcoming whinny whenever she came into view. She would win all the Pony Club competitions and be chosen for the team. Somehow she kept thinking of all this happening with Birdie, yet she knew Birdie was impossible. Birdie had cost a lot of money and belonged to the irascible Mrs Prebble and no-one was supposed to ride her.

Everyone was terribly nice to her for the rest of the day, even Hugh, who said she could ride Cascade (only she didn't want to; Cascade was pig-headed, just like Hugh). With extraordinary timing, Roma Glade's mother rang up in the evening with the news that they had sold a prize pig and decided to use the money to buy Jones for Roma. 'At last! We've messed you about so long – I'm sure you'll be so relieved we've made our minds up after all this shilly-shallying!'

Joan Hawes made all the right noises, but when she put the phone down she said, exasperated,

'What timing! Just when he would have done for Rowan!'

But Rowan, strangely, felt a great sense of relief. She did not want Jones; he was too easy. He was everyone's pony. A 'press-button' pony, they called him. She wanted a pony that would go better for her than it would for anyone else – like only Charlie could get Out of the West round a cross-country course without being carted, and only Hugh could get Cascade to jump clear rounds. She wanted a challenge. Josephine knew this.

'What now?' she said to Rowan in the evening when the ponies were all turned out, save Swallow, who was to be collected in the morning. Rowan was sitting in his manger, talking to him, not having to be brave any more. Tears streamed down her cheeks. Josephine found her when she came back from a ride on Wilfred.

'It's a good home, after all. He'll be well looked after. They're quite well known on the jumping circuit, the Truggs.'

'I know.'

'It's not like he belonged to some idiots, who don't know anything. They've got two grooms and several horses.'

'I know.'

Rowan remembered that Josephine, who was brilliant, didn't have her own horse either. And she never moaned. She leaned over the door, pulling her long blond hair loose and shaking it out. She wore an old brown jersey and her cream jodhpurs with holes in the knees, yet she looked as elegant as always.

'You've got the money. You can buy another pony. Your mother might give you a bit more, to get a decent one, if you ask her.'

Rowan did not answer.

'Come on, Rowan, it's not the end of the world. You'll still see him around. Ponies are always getting outgrown and passed on, it's a fact of life. You just have to get used to it.'

'I know.'

She had got used to the idea by now, but she couldn't get used to her new idea. Birdie.

'I—' She couldn't get it out.

'What is it?'

'I would like—' Her voice failed her. But she knew Josephine, of them all, would understand.

'I want Birdie.'

'Birdie! Heavens, Rowan, you go looking for trouble!'

'I like her.'

'She went well for you. But – oh, Rowan! She's nearly as difficult as Swallow – in a different way, I grant you. And her price! Mrs Prebble paid two and a half thousand for her. That cheque for Swallow – it's only a quarter of that! Your mother'll never pay that much, will she?'

'I shouldn't think so.'

'If you ask Mrs Prebble, I suppose she might let you ride her until she's sold. Or until she decides what she's going to do with her.'

'Am I being really stupid?'

'Yes.'

'But I liked riding her. Better than any of the others. She felt—' Rowan couldn't think of the word. 'Slippery' was the word she remembered, but that wasn't right.

'Sensitive?' Josephine suggested.

'Yes!'

'You're a very sensitive rider. Perhaps you felt she responded to you? Matty wasn't right for her; she was too forceful, she asked too much. And Lizzie couldn't get together with her at all. Perhaps she is right for you, Rowan, who knows?'

Josephine smiled, and Rowan for the first time that day felt that all was not completely lost. Josephine didn't completely throw out the idea.

Josephine understood what she scarcely understood herself.

'Do you want me to see what I can do?'

Rowan looked up in astonishment. 'You think—? I'm not just being really idiotic?'

'Well, fairly idiotic. But it just might – might – work.' Josephine smiled, and then her smile turned off and she said severely, 'If it doesn't, you'll be in a worse way than ever, won't you? Is it worth the risk?'

Rowan didn't answer.

'You make it so hard for yourself!' But then the cool face softened again. Josephine leaned against the door, gazing into space. Then she said, 'Perhaps – if we ask Mrs Prebble – she might lease you Birdie, for long enough to see if you can get on with her. And then, if you do, you could buy her. And if you don't – well, you will have learned sense, and be ready to opt for something suitable.'

'Oh, please – could you ask? And not let the others think I am – am—' She supposed the word was conceited. The others were so brilliant and she was such a duffer; they would think her conceited that she thought she could ride Birdie successfully.

'All right, nut-case. I'll stick up for you.'

The enormous price-tag on Birdie was something Rowan thought she could forget about for the moment, for it was very likely she would never get to the point of actually being able to ride Birdie well enough. Josephine laughed and went in for her supper, and Rowan stayed with Swallow until it was nearly dark.

'I'd rather have you, all the same,' she said. She felt slightly guilty that she was thinking of the next before Swallow had actually gone. She sometimes felt she got things wrong all the time. Perhaps she should try and be more like Hugh, sure he was always right even when it was patently obvious that he wasn't. He always bounced up like a rubber ball.

But Swallow's going hurt badly enough to make her forget all her plans for the future. When the horse-box came for him the next morning she stayed well away and lay on her bed, howling, until her mother told her to come and visit the house-agent with her about buying what they called 'the shop'. Her mother had thought it might be rather fun doing it up. 'Take my mind off things,' she said, meaning the divorce and the hurt and the sense of failure. She had been very low for a few months, but now seemed to be getting a lot more cheerful. Rowan was chastened by thinking how preoccupied she had been with her potty pony problems, and forced herself to turn her mind on to what was now interesting her mother: kitchens and lavatories and central heating. The shop was the only house for sale in Long Bottom, and the thought of moving out to another village beyond bicycling range of High Hawes was horrific, so it made a lot of sense to be enthusiastic. Actually the shop seemed more and more possible the more they examined it. The room that would be Rowan's, at the back, had a view straight up the pony fields and into the back yard of High Hawes – fantastic! – and when the house agent pointed out to Pauline Watkins that she could turn the house round and make the back the living-room, opening into the garden, and the front – the shop – into a kitchen-dining room, instead of vice versa as it was at the moment, everything started to take shape. Excitement quickened.

'Why, I think it could be really sweet! And we could spend money on the improvements when it's so cheap.'

And the stable, Rowan thought with a glow – I can scrub it all out and paint it inside and make it for Birdie to come to sometimes! She got as excited as her mother. They went out for supper in a smart place that night and celebrated the future.

'It doesn't do to dwell on what's past, what can't be helped. On with the next thing, I say,' her mother said.

She wasn't really thinking of Swallow, but it worked for him too.

Mrs Prebble was invited to call, to discuss 'a plan for Birdie'. Joan Hawes shooed everyone out of the kitchen. Only Josephine was to stay and do the deal. Charlie had taken Out of the West to an event, which Josephine said was a good thing as he wasn't very keen on their good idea. He didn't want to be beholden to Mrs Prebble, he said. Leasing was a messy idea. 'Oh, rubbish, not with a good insurance cover,' Josephine countered. 'She'll say you're ruining her, and insurance only covers injury.' And Josephine said quietly, 'Rowan wouldn't ruin any pony, you know that.' Rowan felt proud to have Josephine's trust, but couldn't help being frightened by her own ambition. If Mrs Prebble had been a kindly old soul, like Auntie Millie – 'Of course, darling, see how you get on with her! What a splendid idea! How lovely!'

But Mrs Prebble wasn't like that. She had flaring nostrils and dark, suspicious eyes. She had a haughty, upper-class manner and could be extraordinarily rude. She had been a brilliant rider herself in her heyday but now seemed embittered and without laughs (even before Matty's accident).

Mr Prebble supplied the money, but was only interested in golf himself and was rarely seen at a horse event.

When she arrived she disappeared into the house, leaving Matty out in the yard on her crutches, which she handled with considerable aplomb. Her right leg trailed dispiritingly and wouldn't be much good, Rowan could see, for a bicycle, but a nice quiet pony . . . the thought of having to be taken everywhere by Mrs Prebble was really depressing.

'Can I have a go?' Hugh asked.

Matty handed the crutches over and leaned against the stable wall.

'What's this about Birdie?' she asked as Hugh went lurching away.

'Rowan wants her,' Lizzie said.

'To try her,' Rowan corrected, blushing scarlet. She could tell by the way they all looked at her that they thought she was out of her mind.

But Matty just said, 'She's no good to us. I don't want her.'

'Don't you want to ride again?' Shrimp asked.

Lizzie and Rowan felt embarrassed at Shrimp's indiscretion, but Matty only laughed and said, 'Not Birdie anyway.'

Then she said, 'I would like a horse of my

own. But it doesn't exist, what I want.'

'Why?'

'I don't want a dumb squit, but that's all I can ride now. I've always ridden class horses. I'd rather not bother if I can't, you see.'

Her words were swanky but true, and the way her voice dropped on the last sentence sounded apologetic. Rowan saw that her idea of a bicycle-pony was not going to appeal.

'But it's awfully boring, stuck like this,' Matty said.

They didn't know what to say, feeling awkward. But Hugh came swinging back and shouted, 'I say, this is great! How fast can you go, Matty?'

'Give them to me!'

She showed him, and they all had a go, and Hugh got one of the Pony Club stop-watches out of the tack-room and they all went round the yard being timed. Matty was miles the best; even Hugh couldn't touch her time. Lizzie put out some cavalletti and they tried it with jumps, but Shrimp fell flat on her face and cut her chin and when Mrs Prebble came out with Josephine they were all in the tack-room putting wound powder on her. Matty went out to deflect trouble.

'Have you sold her?'

'No, but if she suits, Mrs Watkins will buy her.'

'Mrs Watkins!'

Rowan couldn't help overhearing the astonishment in Matty's voice. Nobody thought it was going to work, she could see that. Only Josephine held out a faint hope. And even Mrs Prebble's announcement was scary. Where was her mother going to find the money, even if it did work out? Rowan wondered how on earth she had managed to get herself in such a mess.

Mrs Prebble drove off with Matty, and Josephine said to her, 'Cheer up, Rowan! It went well. She agreed to lend her, as long as we insure her – and with an option to buy at the end of the summer holidays.'

Rowan tried to look pleased, but the old, cold fear of failure seemed to grip harder than ever. Whatever had she done?

'Dad'll never pay that money,' she mumbled.

'Rowan!'

Josephine's voice was stern. Rowan raised her eyes nervously.

'Your father is a businessman. Birdie is worth that money if you can ride her. It's up to you. She's only young. Your father will buy her and make a profit when you've grown out of her, because you'll make a good pony into an even better one!

You told me once that money is all your father thinks about. So where's your resolve?'

'It's – it's—'

'Look at me, Rowan!'

Rowan looked. Josephine's eyes were flinty.

'You will do it. You've got to do it, haven't you? There's no alternative.'

CHAPTER SIX

'I don't know why I get myself into such muddles,' Rowan said to Babar. Babar was the only person she could confide in now, all the Haweses except Josephine thinking she was potty. Even dear Charlie did not approve, because he hated being involved with Mrs Prebble.

And she hadn't dared tell her mother yet that at the end of the summer she was going to have to fork out £2500 to keep Birdie.

'Aye, you're a right 'un,' Babar said, and laughed. But kindly. 'That's some fair price, eh?'

Rowan said, 'You know they want to buy another horse for Matty?'

'She can't ride no horse now!'

'No, well, the right horse. Matty herself said she

would ride the right horse. Mrs Prebble said if Charlie found her the right horse for Matty, she would let us have Birdie.'

'For nothing?'

'Well, for much less, she said.'

'I reckon she said it because she knew there ain't no right 'orse for Matty. That's wishful thinking, that is. Unless she wants my ole Diamond. 'E's quiet enough.'

'Well, I don't think so.' Rowan thought it would be imprudent to repeat that Matty didn't want 'a dumb squit', which was an exact description of Diamond.

'If I were you,' Babar said, 'I'd get on and enjoy myself. No use worryin' over what might never 'appen. You ride Birdie and show 'em, and your ma'll marry a rich farmer and come he'll stump up to make you 'appy.'

'You think?' Rowan couldn't help smiling.

'Well, look at it this way. You're better off than Matty?'

'Oh yes!'

'You got what you wanted?'

'Yes.'

'Well then.'

Put that way, there was no argument. Babar's stolid philosophy pulled Rowan together. For the time being, Birdie was hers.

'Well,' said her mother, 'that's very lucky for you! Such a pretty pony! And Mrs Prebble says you can have her for your own?'

'To see if I get on with her. With an option to buy, if I do.'

'That's very generous. I'm sure we'll be able to buy her if she's suitable.'

Even then, Rowan could not bring herself to mention the price. As Babar said, why worry about what might never happen? For the moment, Birdie was hers.

'Shall we go for a ride?' Lizzie asked her when she went up on her bicycle. Rowan had missed the day of Swallow's departure, and the sight of his empty box – although she was prepared for it – gave her a fresh pang of grief.

'Yes!' It was what she most needed, to think ahead, put Birdie in Swallow's place.

They went down the field to catch the ponies. Birdie, not used to coming to work, was surprised to be wanted, but made no demur as Rowan flipped the head-collar round behind her ears. She had a long walking stride and Rowan had to almost run to keep up with her.

She tied her up in her box and groomed her. Her summer coat was just about through, and Rowan's vigorous brushing revealed it, smooth and shining, beneath the mud and old hair. The light, bright bay turned to black round about her knee and hock joints so that she had black legs, and gleaming white stockings behind gave her a showy appearance. As she was beautifully put together this accentuated her presence. She was kind in the stable, but quite different from Swallow, gentler and much less pushy. She had a way of looking into the distance, as if she were listening to something, ears pricked up, and her eyes were soft and purple-dark and unfathomable. Rowan laid her hand on the hard muscle of her neck. What did ponies think about? When you stared into their eyeballs you could not tell. Did they care who owned them? Did they know how badly you wanted them to make it all come right?

Rowan didn't think they did.

Birdie's real name was Bird in the Wilderness, she remembered. Perhaps that was what she was, until now. Perhaps she was waiting to find her way out.

She tacked up and led Birdie out into the yard. Josephine and Charlie had gone out in the horse-box and there was no sign of Hugh or Shrimp. It was a still, grey day, not cold, and the hedges were full in leaf and the hawthorn just beginning to flower, with its thick, summery smell. A little shiver of excitement – pleasure or fear? – made Rowan's hands tremble on the reins as she sat up on Birdie, waiting for Lizzie. She could hear her own heart beating. Yet she was only going for a hack, for heaven's sake! What was wrong with her?

They set off cautiously up the lane. 'Better not go on the downs, until you are used to her more,' Lizzie said wisely. It occurred to both of them, although neither voiced it, that they hadn't asked if they could go out. Deep down, Rowan had a strong idea that she would only be allowed to ride in the school at first, if she asked, and not asking was instinctive.

Birdie walked on calmly with her long, easy stride, so that Lizzie had to keep trotting to keep up. Fable, Lizzie's pony, was common compared to Birdie, but kind and generous. She had no vices at all and Lizzie loved not being scared. With good feeding and plenty of work, Fable had filled out and got her spirit back, hardly recognizable as the sad little plodder they had bought from the riding school. (Nearly all the Haweses' animals had come cheaply from poor homes – 'Only ones we can afford,' Charlie said cheerfully.)

Birdie was so different from Swallow that Rowan couldn't stop being amazed. She felt much more like a horse, although she was only half a hand higher, and she was much narrower and much smoother and her mouth was so light she hardly needed a touch on the reins to turn or stop. Swallow had needed quite a lot of yanking, which had never had much effect. When she trotted, she was so smooth Rowan scarcely had to rise in the saddle.

'She's rather spooky, remember,' Lizzie warned, and no sooner had she said it than Birdie gave a violent jink sideways across the road, and Rowan was pitched over her shoulder. She almost didn't fall off, her foot desperately hooked over the saddle, but in the end it was a very slow-motion fall, depositing her quite gently on the tarmac. She held on to the reins, and Birdie started cropping the grass verge.

'Whatever was that for?' Rowan asked indignantly.

'That gateway – the notice,' Lizzie said. There was a white notice which said HALL FARM, not at all terrifying as far as Rowan could see.

'You have to watch out for things in advance. She always does it. You get to see things before she does – even cigarette packets.'

While Rowan was hopping about getting back on, Lizzie lay down with the back of her head on

Fable's rump and laughed, 'You can't do this with Birdie. You can't relax.'

So, now she was learning!

'What else does she do that I ought to know about?'

'The spooks is her worst. You never know. Sometimes she spins round and tries to go home when you're not expecting it. Sometimes when you're cantering she puts her head up in a horrid way, or sometimes down, so that she sort of disappears from in front of you. She doesn't bolt like Swallow, but she gets quite excited when you go fast.'

'Does she buck?'

'No.'

Something to be thankful for!

They continued on their way, following a track down into the next valley, where Jerry Patterson and the racehorses lived. Then they had come so far that to go back by the road was miles.

'We'll have to go back over the down,' Lizzie said dubiously. 'It'll be all right if we walk.'

'We could canter up,' Rowan said. 'Some of the way.'

'I suppose so.'

Rowan was rather cross with Lizzie for being so careful, as if she were convinced that Birdie's rider was completely incapable. But everything that had happened so far (apart from the spook – and she was ready for spooks now) filled Rowan with a confidence and joy that she really had never felt on Swallow. Yes, she might be tricky, but Birdie liked her – Rowan knew she did. She could sense it. Rowan felt at one with Birdie, even if she wasn't much of a rider. (Yet.) So when the chalk track up the hill out of the valley petered out on to the lovely down turf Rowan turned in her saddle and shouted, 'I'm going to canter.'

She scarcely had to tell Birdie. The mare knew, springing straight into a canter from a walk. Rowan managed to go with her, feeling a great surge of adrenalin rushing through her body, half fear, half excitement, at the amazing feel of Birdie in full flight, so strong and smooth and willing. She didn't bolt like Swallow, nor did she put her head up, but rather bent her power to Rowan's message on the reins, very kind, even when so fast. And fast she was! Her long thoroughbred legs swept her up the hill, leaving Fable toiling far behind, for all she was much fitter than Birdie. Like a racehorse, thought Rowan, almost delirious with joy at the feel of it. She had never, ever, felt this heaven on Swallow. She wished for a heady moment that there were great jumps ahead of them that the mare would take in her stride, for she knew – she just *knew* – that they would fly over them without hesitation.

As it was, Birdie wasn't fit and came back to Rowan immediately she decided to slow down, her breathing coming flared through her nostrils so the membrane showed red. As she dropped to a walk she flitched her black tail and dropped her nose as if to say, that was good. Rowan leaned forward and stroked her hot neck.

Fable came toiling up and Lizzie shouted, 'I thought she'd taken off with you!'

'No, she never – she's just so fast. I never felt she was out of control.'

After that they walked all the way home, anxious to show that they had been very quiet and good. Rowan rather thought she would get a wigging, but nothing would take away her feeling of triumph, that Birdie was going to be right for her. She now knew what everyone had tried to tell her about Swallow. She had never listened to them. She had always been frightened of riding Swallow. But Birdie—!

She did get a wigging, from both Josephine and Charlie, but even they noticed the look of bliss on her face and had a laugh when they left her.

'At least she's still in one piece. What a case!'

Charlie said. 'Talk about single-minded!'

'People like that succeed,' Josephine said.

'If they don't kill themselves first.'

'Hark who's talking!'

'I just wish Birdie didn't belong to that Prebble woman. She's perfectly capable of throwing a spanner in the works, however well it goes for Rowan. I wouldn't trust her farther than I could throw her.'

'The answer to that is to get poor Matty riding again. Then Mrs Prebble won't give a toss for what happens to Birdie. But I can't see how, exactly – I thought side-saddle, perhaps, with her right leg being useless. But the right horse . . .'

'One in a million. They still want pure class, and yet utter reliability – docility. Rare as ice in the desert.'

'It's got to be very special for Matty.'

'Yes. And I'm not wasting time looking for it.'

It seemed amazing to Rowan that something in her horse life was going right at last. Her colossal gamble had come off – Birdie *did* go for her; they suited each other. Twice a week she had a lesson in the school with Josephine, and other days, as the evenings grew longer, she rode out with Lizzie and Shrimp, and even Hugh, whose antics on Cascade did not disturb Birdie as they had Swallow. It was true she had to watch out for the mare's spooks, and sometimes she did fall off, taken unawares. She also found that Birdie could sometimes get impatient and silly if schooled for too long. Josephine said she was a bit of a baby and had been spoilt in her youth, and it was best to humour her, and make the lessons short. But the schooling was more to teach Rowan to ride better rather than to teach Birdie anything, so sometimes Josephine would give her a lesson on Wilfred, or the Armchair, to show her how different horses felt and how differently they needed to be ridden. Rowan, now she had her confidence, felt she was improving at an amazing rate. Josephine must have thought so too, for she said one evening, 'If you don't watch out, Auntie Millie will have you in the Pony Club team.'

'But—' Confident as she felt, Rowan knew she was far from being a Hawes.

'Birdie's a very good jumper.'

Rowan wasn't sure if her new confidence stretched to competing against the likes of Hugh – or Tom Thug. She wasn't a natural show-off like Hugh. But the season for shows was upon them, and Charlie was taking Hugh and Lizzie and Shrimp in the horse-box . . .

'You can enter for novice jumping,' Lizzie said. 'Birdie's still a novice; I never won anything on her and nor did Matty – she never had time before she got hurt.'

The others took it for granted that she would come. Josephine said gently, 'Not if you don't want to. But I think you're ready. It's not affiliated, only a potty little show for charity. Otty runs it.'

Otty was one of the Pony Club instructors. She had a young horse called Hadrian, and was funny and nice. Rowan was persuaded.

'It's not Wembley,' Lizzie said in scathing tones, when she saw Rowan's nervousness.

It was all right for them – they had been to shows since they were born. Shrimp had almost lived in shows until recently, having ridden show-ponies for rich owners. Charlie was taking Out of the West to jump, for practice, and Priscilla was going to jump Wilfred in the Novice Horse. With six animals entered, Josephine agreed to take the trailer for two of them, as the horse-box didn't take more than four comfortably, only if illegally squashed up. Everyone took it quite for granted, but Rowan was awake all the night before, and felt sick with nerves when she got up. Lizzie couldn't believe it, seeing her so pale and quiet.

'It's just the pottiest show – however can you be

nervous? Birdie jumps far better than Fable and I'm not nervous.'

Rowan tried to be cool. The two of them bagged to go with Josephine. Rowan did not want to be unnerved by swanky Hugh, who had the Challenge Cup for Junior Jumping newly cleaned and gleaming on his lap, to take back from last year. He nearly didn't clean it, so convinced was he that he was going to win it back again, but his mother made him. At least he wasn't in the same class as Rowan. He was in the Open under 14.2. Cascade was no novice.

It was a sunny day, not too hot. The show was in a big flat farm field beyond the next village, only a few miles away. Rowan's mother was coming in her car with Joan Hawes and a picnic. If Rowan was quiet, nobody else noticed. They parked the lorry and trailer and went off to the Secretary's tent to get their numbers and find out what the opposition was. Otty was in there and pleased to see them.

'Who are you riding, Rowan?' She was curious, giving out the numbers. 'Swallow? Jones?'

'No. Birdie.' Rowan explained what had happened.

'Very interesting. I think she might go very well for you. She needs understanding, that one.'

It was a compliment, but Rowan didn't take it in. The Novice jumps were quite small but arranged in a complicated sort of course with some sharp changes of direction.

'It's a rider course,' Josephine said. 'Not to go too fast, Rowan, and keep your eye on the next jump all the time, that's the best way. The first round isn't against the clock, remember. I'll walk the course with you.'

Josephine showed her where to take it steady, how to make a straight approach, where she could cut corners if she went into the timed jump-off.

'Watch the others. You can learn from their mistakes. And think of it as a lesson, not an ordeal! You've never done it before, but you've got a pony who loves jumping. She's not going to refuse unless you get her into a complete muddle, and I'm sure you won't do that.'

At least the Novice class was first, thank goodness. Lizzie was jumping Fable in it, and Jones arrived in the collecting ring with his new owner, Roma Glade. She came up to Rowan and said, 'Cor, that's Birdie, isn't it?'

'Yes.'

'Cor, rather you than me.' Roma, the pig farmer's daughter, was not noted for her way with words, and reminded Rowan that poor Birdie, although it had in no way been her fault, was still regarded as the pony that nearly killed Matty Prebble. A small crowd was collecting as the class was announced, and Rowan saw her mother at the ropes, looking more frightened than she felt herself. Neither Roma nor Lizzie seemed to be bothered at all, and pushed in to go early.

They both went clear. Rowan knew that Birdie could jump far better than both their ponies and if she made a mess of it, it would be her fault. She would have no excuse. Her number was called and she turned towards the ring entrance.

'Don't start until you hear the hooter,' Josephine warned her.

Birdie was excited, knowing what it was all about, and needed no urging as Rowan trotted her in a circle while the judge took her number and gave them the hooter. Now she was started, Rowan found that everything seemed much less alarming and the first jump looked only knee-high and positively beckoned across the soft green turf. Birdie wanted to go faster than she did, but Rowan wasn't sure about whether she ought to rein her in as she approached the jump – decided not to, and Birdie flew over it so big that Rowan was nearly thrown out of the saddle. Half out – and then she wasn't ready to gather the mare together on the other side as she had intended . . . Rowan bit her tongue and almost panicked as Birdie bore down on the next set of rails at a very fast canter. She took a pull out of a sense of self-preservation, nothing to do with horsemanship, and Birdie came back fractionally, bounced up and down on the spot – or so it seemed – and then plunged wildly over the rails. Rowan heard nothing fall, but thought she had probably gone deaf as well as stupid – her senses seemed to have left her. Where was the next jump? She had no idea.

Birdie was now heading for the ropes and looked set to jump them too, but suddenly Josephine was there, hissing, 'The red wall on your left! Slow down!'

Rowan, anguished at the thought of being found wanting, desperately pulled her wits together. Charlie must be watching too! The thought was like ice on her fevered brain. She saw the next jump clearly and the one beyond it, and pulled Birdie gently, firmly, out of her sprawling canter and back to a trot, collected her exactly as Josephine had taught her in the school and, three strides away, kicked her on to jump the wall. Perfectly!

Now Rowan saw the course ahead of her, the order of jumps neatly in her brainbox, knew exactly how she must calm Birdie and present her straight and collected. Suddenly she was in charge and – wonder of wonders! – enjoying herself. Birdie, although hyped up, was still controllable, quite unlike Swallow whom she could never have jumped in public. Well, fairly controllable . . . Rowan knew they were going too fast, but safely fast, or so she thought. She just had to steer. Nothing fell, and they flew through the finish and did two circles to pull up.

Josephine was severe. 'If those jumps had been anything at all, you'd have knocked half of them down.'

Rowan listened to her but, now it was over, she was so fantastically thrilled with the feeling that she hardly took it in. She had gone clear!

'But for the grace of God—' Josephine said darkly. 'Much too fast!'

'I couldn't help it.'

'You've got to help it, muttonhead! The jump-off will be against the clock, but if you go even faster you'll end up through the ropes. This is your first show, Rowan – it's a practice for the future. Much better in the jump-off to be under control and riding well all the way and coming fourth or fifth, than to win in a crazy, lucky gallop. Of course Birdie can do it – we all know that – but you were no help to her at all.'

'You've got to be a credit to us,' Hugh said smugly. 'Nobody's going to ask Josephine for lessons if you're any advert.'

It was Hugh saying this that put steel into Rowan's soul. The pig!

They drew lots for order of going for the jump-off. There were about a dozen clears and Rowan drew near the end, after both Lizzie and Roma.

Josephine said, 'Don't think about winning this time. Think about doing a copybook round. Show them you can.' Show me, she meant.

Rowan could see how Lizzie, even though Fable was no great jumper, got her round very fast by pure riding. No jerks or skids, but economical turns, perfectly controlled. Fable was not a natural goer, and had to be kicked on all the way, but she did a fast clear. Roma on Jones tried to emulate her but, without Lizzie's experience, got a refusal when her attempted fast turn got her into the jump all wrong. But Jones was a real trier and did well in spite of his rider's over-keen riding. Rowan saw that that was what she mustn't do.

As it was her turn to go, she got a glimpse of Charlie turning round from chatting to someone to watch her. It stiffened her resolve – she would do exactly as Josephine said! Don't think of winning. Then she saw Hugh grinning, and her resolve changed to deep indignation. No advert indeed! So she rode out in a great wash of excitement and whizzing adrenalin, not knowing what on earth she was going to do.

At least she now knew the course – the same, luckily. The thing was to go fast between jumps, but come back to jump them all in hand, and be ready on landing to turn quickly. But she wasn't yet secure enough on landing to gather the pony together quickly enough. She still felt on landing that she was jolly lucky to have made it, and she needed several strides to congratulate herself and sort herself out again. Of course, while she was doing this, Birdie was flying off in the wrong direction. Even so, although in no way as expert as Lizzie, she got a clear round and was only a few seconds slower.

When she came out Josephine was smiling and said, 'Jolly good effort, Rowan. For your first show that was brilliant.'

Hugh gave her a sort of pitying sneer, and Charlie said, 'You rode that very well. Well done.'

For this accolade, her day was made. She came fourth. Lizzie was third and two people they didn't know were first and second. Her rosette was green and glittered proudly on Birdie's browband. Rowan leaned forward and put her cheek against the hard, sweaty neck. 'You're wonderful, Birdie. It's only me that's no good. I promise you I'll get better, and then you'll win.'

Her mother was thrilled, and Rowan, after all her cowardly fears, found that the day was suddenly all sunshine and she went to the Secretary's tent and collected a sheaf of schedules for future shows.

Shrimp won the under 12.2 Open and Hugh won the 14.2 Open and got his cup back. Grudgingly, Rowan had to admit that he was brilliant. He had his photo taken by the newspapers, one hand on the cup that he had so unwillingly cleaned the night before. He wasn't nearly as thrilled with his win as she was with her fourth.

'Oh, he's such a bighead,' Lizzie sympathized.

They were going to watch Charlie jump Out of the West, but Rowan went back to the horse-box first to make sure Birdie was all right. She had her hay-net and a summer sheet on and was tied outside the trailer with Fable.

There was a man looking at her with a young girl at his side. When Rowan hitched the hay-net up better, he said to her, 'Is this the pony that came fourth in the Novice?'

'Yes.'

'Is she yours?'

'Yes.'

'You're not thinking of selling her, I suppose?'

'No!'

'I like her very much,' the man said. 'Just the sort we're looking for. If she does come on the market . . .' He handed Rowan a card and smiled. 'No offence, I hope?'

Perhaps he was nervous of the glare Rowan gave him. He retreated, leaving Rowan with a wildly beating pulse. It was almost as bad as all the uncertainties with Swallow, owning Birdie and yet not owning her. She did not even look at the card, but shoved it deep into her jodhpur pocket. Thank goodness Mrs Prebble wasn't around! Just as well none of the others had overheard either . . . the offer was something she was going to keep to herself.

But, when she went to watch Charlie, and stood beside Josephine at the ringside, she remembered that her two heroes did not really own the horses they rode either. Prissy had jumped Wilfred in the Novice and knocked down the triple bar, which made Josephine mad – 'The stupid girl – *legs*, for heaven's sake! She rides like a mashed potato!' But, Rowan thought, if Josephine was riding him he could get round the Open without much trouble. She jumped him at home and Wilfred jumped splendidly for her.

But Out of the West – he was another matter. He was so super-powered that it took all Charlie's expertise to keep him calm enough to jump. As a three-day event horse, he had to be equally good at dressage, cross-country and show-jumping. He settled fairly well for dressage and his superb paces and Charlie's incredibly tactful riding got him quite good marks in spite of lack of experience. His power and enthusiasm in cross-country made him one of the best, but the same enthusiasm in a constricted show-jumping ring tended to lead to his downfall. He got so excited at seeing the jumps that he couldn't wait to fly over them and, so long and powerful was his stride, he was on to the next out of control – just like me, Rowan thought – and apt to send the poles flying. Charlie was trying to teach him to listen to instructions but Out of the West was a bighead like Hugh and hated to be told.

'He's so brilliant cross-country,' Josephine sighed, 'and throws everything away show-jumping. He's just got to learn. Poor Charlie!'

Mr Hicks had come to watch and stood by the ropes beside them. He was gloriously rich, Rowan remembered, sneaking him a look to see if he had a sweet, kind face and might buy Birdie for her out of kindness of heart. But he had a face like flint, hard with doing big deals in the city. Rowan remembered her father saying that kind people didn't get rich very often. 'You have to be ruthless to make megabucks,' he had said. (He was fairly rich and fairly ruthless, in Rowan's opinion, but now that he had two families to support – the secretary had three children, it transpired – he kept saying suddenly that he was poor.)

The difference between her and Charlie was that, whatever Out of the West did, Charlie stayed with him, and in the jump, however wild, Charlie was like a part of him, never jabbing his mouth or budging one inch out of his perfect position. Now she had tried it herself, Rowan was in even more awe of Charlie's expertise. Calming, calming – he never got cross or too strict, letting the horse run on enough to make him happy, yet sensitively, so tactfully, collecting him enough to make a good presentation at the jump.

Josephine said, 'If you collect him too much he sulks and knocks them down. He's so bold! But he's learning, slowly. This sort of outing is just what he needs.'

He didn't win because he knocked the last triple bar flying, but Charlie was very pleased with him. He came out of the ring patting his neck and saying nice things to him, and grinned happily at old flint-face Hicks.

'Great, eh? He'd have flattened the lot a couple of months ago.'

'Well, if you say so,' Mr Hicks said tetchily.

'It takes time.'

'You're always saying that.'

No congratulations or encouragement . . . 'He's cross because Prissy didn't win,' Josephine whispered. 'And that was no fault of the horse's. Only her feebleness.'

But, as if she didn't think any of this, she went cheerily up to Mr Hicks and said, 'A great round, don't you think, Mr Hicks, considering he's only a baby? He must have a real future. You know how to pick them, eh?'

Such blatant flattery – even Rowan could see it a mile off – worked wonders on Mr Hicks. A thin smile cracked his lips and he was obviously pleased to be admired by the girl turning her beautiful clear-blue eyes on him. It was completely out of character for Josephine to act in that way, but it had the right effect. Their livelihood depended on Mr Hicks for the time being and they were defending it valiantly with their deference.

When they were in the lorry going home, Rowan sat next to Charlie and he said, 'Stupid old twit – I don't know how I keep my cool! Josephine's brilliant.'

Rowan realized he had worse troubles than she had with Birdie, with far more at stake if he lost his horse. She told herself this, but it was no real comfort. When she brushed Birdie down in her box, she kept thinking of her having a second home in the stable behind the shop, where she would be truly, utterly hers . . . and they would go to shows and she would learn to control her and ride like Charlie, and when someone offered to buy her she could turn and say coolly, 'A million wouldn't be enough to buy this mare.'

'Oh, Birdie, you are so lovely!' And she flung her arms round the mare's neck. Birdie nudged her for a polo mint, and then Rowan thought of Swallow and felt terrible. Then she saw the green rosette lying in the manger and felt wonderful. And she laughed, and nearly cried, and went home for her tea.

CHAPTER SEVEN

Pauline Watkins bought the shop and a builder made the required improvements. The builder had a black bathroom suite cheap from a demolition job so they had that installed with gold taps and red shower curtains.

'Great, isn't it?' Pauline Watkins was thrilled and Rowan thought, she'd never have dared have a wacky bathroom like that when her husband had been around. It would have been pink or avocado. Like her bedroom, there was a view up the pony field and no frosted glass – 'Whoever's going to watch us having a bath, for heaven's sake?'

As she had suspected, Rowan soon learned that there was no money over from doing up the cottage. Her father disputed all the bills, in spite of having sold their smart house in the village for plenty of money.

Her mother said, 'Half each, it isn't a fortune,' as if to defend him.

Rowan plucked up courage to tell her mother Birdie's price.

'Do you think he'll buy her for me in the autumn?' The lease agreed with Mrs Prebble was up at the end of October.

Pauline Watkins was stunned. 'At that figure! I should think it's highly unlikely! However can she be worth as much as that?'

'It's what Mrs Prebble paid for her. She just wants her money back.'

'But what a lot! The Haweses sold her for that?'

'Yes. They are horse dealers, after all, and Charlie put the price up because he didn't want Mrs Prebble to buy her. But she did, all the same. Birdie's got what they call potential.'

'Haven't we all, given the chance?' Pauline said rather bitterly. 'Oh, darling, I can't see him paying that much! Half, perhaps. He does love you, after all.'

Rowan thought there was no price on love. Wrong again. She could see her mother was very cast down.

'There's no extra cash. I'm earning a bit with the cooking but only enough to barely keep us, there's nothing to save. We might hit the big time, but not before October, I shouldn't think.'

She did sandwiches and local dinner parties with Joan Hawes and they seemed to enjoy themselves working together. They were both very good cooks.

Rowan had come across the card in her jods pocket from the man who had offered to buy Birdie at her first show and, without saying why, asked Lizzie if she knew who he was.

'Oh, yes,' said Lizzie. 'Big show-jumper. Hickstead and all that. Charlie knows him.'

Had he said anything to Charlie? But Rowan knew she was safe until October, even if they were queuing up to buy Birdie after that. And it didn't help that she was steadily improving and that the green rosette tacked to her bedroom wall (something else her father wouldn't have allowed) was quite soon joined by several others: red, blue, and yellow. In spite of her inadequate riding, Birdie was doing clear rounds, and their confidence was growing show by show. Rowan thought of nothing else. She was deeply committed to Birdie and her new life and everyone said exactly what they hadn't said about Swallow –

'You two seem made for each other.'

By the summer holidays Birdie was out of the Novice classes and was jumping against Hugh – and Tom Thug. She couldn't beat them, although she came third once.

In spite of Tom Thug being so beastly, worse than Hugh, Rowan saw that he and Swallow were extremely well-suited. Tom Thug was a laconic, undemonstrative boy with, as far as Rowan could see, no redeeming features at all. He sat hunched on Swallow in the collecting ring, watching his fellow competitors going over the practice bar with his pale, spiky-lashed eyes saying nothing behind his sportsman's glasses. If Swallow fidgeted he growled at him and Swallow stood still. Rowan had never got Swallow to stand still. Swallow wore a twisted snaffle and some severe gadgetry with which Tom Thug was able to control him – although Tom was no more severe on him than was necessary and was undeniably a very strong and able rider, as good as Hugh. He usually beat Hugh, which made Hugh furious. Hugh was not a good loser, especially as Rowan knew that he had had his eye on Swallow for his own after Rowan failed to ride him.

'It's all your fault – showing off on him to the newspaper,' Shrimp said candidly. 'If he'd never had his photo in the paper, the Thugs would never have seen and we'd still have Swallow. And you'd probably be riding him by now because Rowan—' She shrugged and laughed.

'Rowan never would,' Rowan finished for her. She could say it now, without being upset. Swallow, she now saw, was a bit of a thug himself. Birdie was a lady. Swallow's film was to open in London in the autumn, and they were all going to the opening night, amongst the film stars (they hoped).

Just as the summer holidays were starting, Auntie Millie, the Pony Club boss, came to High Hawes to have a chat with Joan Hawes.

'I've got to make up a team for a competition in the holidays. The Barnfield Hill Pony Club is running a One Day Event, and we've got to send a team. Their DC is such a dreadful woman – she's only running it because she thinks she can beat us all. She's got the Truggs, for a start, and that very good gel Melinda Bottomly. She thinks it's all buttoned up. But we've got Hugh and we've also got Rowan now. I just want to know if you think Rowan's ready to be thrown in at the deep end?'

'I would have thought so,' Joan Hawes said. 'She'll shiver and look terrified, of course. She still can't believe it's happening to her, poor mite. But I'm sure Josephine would agree to it. Ask her.'

'Well, I'm banking on it. We stand a chance then. I'm afraid Fable isn't up to it, although of course Lizzie is. I suppose—?'

Joan Hawes laughed. 'No, we're *not* looking for a better pony for Lizzie. Hugh, perhaps, but not Lizzie. She doesn't want to be in your teams, does she? She's happy with Fable.'

'She's no ambition, that girl!'

'We don't all want to be winners, Millie, thank God! There's enough in this family without Lizzie too.'

'No, I can't complain. Pity we haven't got Matty Prebble these days, although at least we've got her pony. What's the situation there, by the way?'

Joan Hawes explained it. 'We can't see poor Rowan keeping Birdie, somehow. Not at that price. Lucy Prebble says she'll do any exchange, or part exchange, if we find a suitable pony for Matty to start riding again, but of course Charlie won't take the risk. If it doesn't turn out perfect we'll get the blame. That woman is such a pain!'

'Oh dear, poor kids! What a muddle.'

Rowan couldn't believe she was being asked to be part of the Pony Club team. Josephine said to her patiently, as if to an idiot, 'It's what happens,

Rowan, if you are successful. You – are – a – success.'

Rowan felt shivery even thinking about it.

'Of course' – more severely, being an instructor, Josephine continued – 'I think it's a little premature, but a brilliant chance. You must take it. Your dressage is easily as good as Hugh's and Tom Thug will have to be brilliant to get decent marks with Swallow, so you should start with an advantage. Then it's up to you.'

'But I haven't done any cross-country!'

'You have round the fields here. But, true, that's where you need the practice. We'll ask Charlie.'

Charlie said amiably, 'We'll take her to Sparrow Farm and have a morning round there. Birdie will love it. The three of us can go, not the others. We can take Jack and Wilfred.'

Sparrow Farm was a cross-country course ten miles away where one paid to practise. It had jumps of varying sizes, to suit novice and experienced horses. When Hugh heard they were going he wanted to come too but Charlie said crushingly, 'You don't want any more practice, idiot. Your pony'll be clapped out by the time of the competition, the way you career about.'

'There's room in the lorry!'

'Not in the cab,' Charlie said. He knew that the last thing Rowan wanted was Hugh's company. He would turn it into a competition from the first fence.

Josephine thought it would be good practice for Priscilla, but they then decided they didn't want their day spoilt by Priscilla's company any more than Hugh's.

'Just us three,' Charlie decided.

Rowan was thrilled to be so privileged. She knew Charlie had the pressure on him from Mr Hicks to start Out of the West in serious competition in the autumn and cross-country practice was useful for him, too. Charlie thought it was too soon, but Mr Hicks paid the bills. It was up to Charlie to make it a success, in spite of his misgivings. He too might lose his horse, just like Rowan, if things didn't go right. Moaning about Mr Hicks, Charlie sighed and said, 'It's a hard life!' then laughed, because they were driving over the downs in their horse-box to go jumping, not standing in a dole queue or working in a car factory or sweltering in the Stock Exchange.

'Money's not everything,' he said.

And Josephine said, 'It is if it means buying Birdie and keeping Jack to make us a living and things like that.'

Charlie changed gear as the lorry started to labour up a hill and his expression changed and he said, 'It's horrible if you start thinking seriously – that our family's bread depends largely on this beast in the back of the lorry jumping cross-country well enough to please old Hicks.'

'Not really,' said Josephine. 'Everyone has to please their employers to keep their jobs.'

'I wish Jack understood that!'

Rowan saw that her Birdie thing was really quite minor beside Charlie's problems. All the same, there was nothing she could do to help him and he refused point-blank to help her.

'No way am I going to get involved in finding Matty a pony! Even for you, dear Rowan.'

'What do you think Matty wants?' Rowan thought she might find one herself if she knew what she was looking for.

Josephine said, 'Matty's growing quite fast. It's got to be fifteen two-ish with a fabulous temperament, impeccable manners and obedience, very good-looking – our Mrs P is a terrible snob about looks – possibly an older horse, with spirit enough not to be boring yet utterly trustworthy. Altogether, a rare beast.'

'What she *ought* to buy is something like our Armchair,' Charlie said, 'but of course she wouldn't have such a common-looking horse in her stables.'

'Quite. After all, looks don't matter a jot if the horse is right for the job,' Josephine said.

Rowan tried to remember the requirements. She would have to look herself. Where on earth to start? Perhaps Lizzie would help her. It was her only chance of keeping Birdie, she could see. But stupid to spoil the day with worrying, when she was out with her two idols to jump dear Birdie cross-country. Who could ask for more bliss than that?

The cross-country course was set in rolling farmland, with a wood in the middle and a water complex, which was what Charlie wanted for Out of the West. The horse was already jumping freely over big fences and ditches, but needed practice with trickier and more unusual obstacles, such as steps and jumps into water. There were large fences for Open horses and, beside them, medium and smaller ones for Novice horses and the likes of Birdie, built in similar style. Hugh had already told Rowan that Cascade had jumped round the course several times, and done the Novice course twice. It was only Lizzie's presence, Rowan thought, that stopped him from saying he'd been round the Open course as well.

'You'll have to take Rowan,' Charlie said to Josephine. Once mounted on Out of the West, his whole attention was occupied.

They saddled up and mounted and rode the horses in, then Charlie went to 'play in the water' and Josephine on Wilfred said she would go round with Rowan.

'Just a jump at a time, very steadily, Rowan. Birdie's done this before – she'll be fine.'

'What about the water?' Hugh had told Rowan about the water complex. The thought of jumping over a fence into water terrified her.

'Birdie's OK. Think positive. She'll do it.'

When someone like Josephine said she'd do it, Rowan believed her. As it was, Birdie set off through the start first. Josephine followed her and they had no trouble. When they came to the lake they pulled up as Out of the West was standing in it.

'Cooling off.' Charlie laughed and rode out. 'He's done them beautifully – the two bottom ones. I'm going to jump the top one and call it a day.'

The top one was, Rowan thought, horrible, with an earth bank built up in front of the water. On top of the bank there was a heavy telegraph pole, not very high but, with the bank, making quite a steep drop into the water. The middle one had a smaller drop and the bottom jump – hers – no drop at all, just a telegraph pole about two feet high immediately in front of the lake.

Birdie flew over it and Rowan was so surprised and pleased she did it again. Nothing to it! Josephine jumped Wilfred over the middle one and then they pulled up to watch Charlie.

'When he's done, you can go round again on your own,' Josephine said. 'Just keep her steady, that's all, no rushing.'

Birdie with her soft mouth was much easier to steady than Swallow. Rowan felt confident and keen to go again. Birdie swung beneath her as she pulled her up out of Charlie's way. She sat beside Josephine and watched Charlie canter Out of the West slowly round the back of the bank, keeping his stride short. The horse, as always, was pulling hard and bounded up the bank with kangaroo-like leaps. But at the top, instead of taking the last leap out wide over the top, he seemed to suddenly lose his confidence. He stopped dead with a snort, then made a half-hearted half-rear to clear the bar, caught his toe on the top and cartwheeled spectacularly over into the lake, landing with a huge splash on his back.

For a moment there was nothing to be seen but

churning spray and flashing iron hooves. Rowan sat paralysed with horror.

'Oh, my God!' Josephine cried out.

She wheeled Wilfred round and trotted sharply round the end of the lake to where Out of the West was set to emerge, streaming water. Charlie was secondary to the valuable horse. With fraught alacrity she caught the trailing reins just in time to stop him galloping off. She leapt off and shouted to Rowan, 'Come and help me!'

Charlie was staggering out of the lake, wet to the skin. Rowan clumped her heels to Birdie's side and cantered over to Josephine who, with one look at Charlie, said, 'Collarbone?'

'Yeah,' said Charlie.

Josephine said to Rowan sharply, 'Get off and hold Wilfred for me.'

Charlie was clutching his shoulder and looking rather white. He said, 'We can't let Jack finish on that.'

'No, I'll take him over it,' Josephine said.

'Get Rowan to give you a lead. I'll hold Wilfred.'

'What, over the top?' Rowan nearly fainted with fright.

Charlie, in spite of everything, laughed. 'No, you twit, the little one!'

He took Wilfred's reins from her, half laughing, half groaning. His left arm wasn't working, and as soon as he had the reins looped over his right arm he went back to holding the injured arm in place. He said to Rowan comfortingly, seeing her fear, 'I've done it twice before. I know the drill.'

'Is it broken?'

'Yes, but it's only a collarbone. They mend quite quickly.'

Rowan thought he was incredibly brave. It put her on her mettle, not to let him down in the cause of Out of the West's schooling.

'Just go like you did before,' Josephine said. 'And we'll follow. It will reassure him, after that fall.'

Rowan gathered Birdie up and cantered her back round the bank. She felt hyped up and had no doubt at all as she faced the lake for the second time. Birdie flew it and the big horse followed her without a hesitation. Rowan turned in her saddle and shouted, 'I'll do the middle one, if you like!'

She did not see the look that passed between Josephine and Charlie. They knew they should stop her, but neither of them did. They both took chances, knew they shouldn't, and still did.

Rowan, in her wonderful new role of

confidence-giver, cantered boldly round the back of the bank again, and faced Birdie for the middle jump. As she approached and saw the drop ahead of her she wondered suddenly what on earth she was doing, gulped, and drove Birdie on. The water seemed awfully far down this time – whatever did the top jump feel like? It was like the high board in the swimming pool; she had stood there but never jumped. This time there was a loud splash as she hit the water and for a moment she thought she was going to go in, pitching over Birdie's shoulder. But her seat was improving all the time and miraculously she stayed in the saddle and was able to canter out in great style before being overtaken by the exuberant Out of the West. Josephine did two circles before she could pull up.

'I feel sure he'd do the top one now!' she shouted at Charlie.

But Charlie shook his head.

'Don't risk it. He's done well. Just cool him off and we'll get home.'

The day hadn't gone as planned, but Rowan felt that Birdie would do anything she asked. Her confidence was increasing all the time. Half of her was thrilled with her success, the other half cast down by Charlie's accident. Josephine had to drive the lorry. She tied Charlie's arm up with Jack's tail-bandage.

'It's not too mucky. I'll drop you off at Casualty and come back in the car later.'

'Losing time now – I can't afford it—'

Charlie, Rowan could see, was now feeling his pain and disappointment, huddled beside her in the cab and looking, strangely, rather like Hugh in one of his bad moods.

'No – well – I'll keep him going for you till it's mended,' Josephine said. 'The rate Rowan's improving I reckon she'll soon be up to it!'

Rowan flushed with pride. At that moment she felt the remark wasn't far-fetched at all. Jumping the middle water had been magical, feeling Birdie's commitment – joy even. The little mare loved it. Yet with Lizzie she had been difficult, and even Matty hadn't liked her. She is *mine*, Rowan thought fiercely, she is *meant* for me. But in her triumph she had to commiserate with Charlie. It was he who had warned that doing anything ambitious with ponies was all ups and downs – huge disappointments followed great triumphs.

'How long will it be, getting better?'

'I can ride again quite soon if I take bute,' he said.

'What's bute?'

'It's a painkiller.'

Josephine laughed and said, 'Painkiller for horses. But lots of riders take it.'

'Don't tell Ma,' Charlie said quickly to Rowan.

'Collarbones are two a penny,' Josephine said. 'But they mend easily because they don't move about like arms and legs. They hurt though. I've only done it once.'

'Ribs hurt most,' Charlie said.

Josephine duly made a detour to the local hospital and pulled up outside the Casualty entrance to let Charlie out. Rowan offered to stop with him, seeing his miserable face, but he told her not to be daft.

'You can do all my work next week if you want to be helpful – mucking out and grooming.'

'Yes, I will!' Rowan breathed.

Charlie laughed, groaned – 'You are a nut, Rowan' – and disappeared through the Casualty door. Out of the West was kicking in the lorry, thinking they had arrived somewhere, but stopped as they drove away.

'Mr Hicks'll be cross,' Josephine sighed. 'Poor Charlie. Jack pulls so hard – only Charlie can get him round a course; I can't. One or two jumps, then after that I can't hold him.'

Rowan knew the feeling well. 'Like me and Swallow.'

'Exactly. They're two of a kind.'

Rowan felt muddled when she got home, on a high with her Birdie feelings but then even more anxious about the future. She wished she wasn't such a worrier. None of the Haweses seemed to worry like she did. Perhaps she got it from her mother. But her mother, in the new cottage, seemed much happier.

'Why don't you clean out that stable?' she suggested. 'Make it nice for Birdie? It would be great for you, having her in the back garden.'

'Only sometimes,' Rowan said. She didn't think Birdie would want to be away from her friends much. And she didn't want to be away from the Hawes. But the thought of her own snug stable at home somehow made her think that she would actually own Birdie one day. But Lizzie told her gloomily that the better she did with Birdie the more easily Mrs Prebble would be able to sell her.

'You win at Barnfield Hill and lots of people will want her.'

'Win! There's no chance of that, not with Tom Thug and Hugh going round. And that Melinda girl.'

'Gel,' said Lizzie.

'I'm dreading it.'

'You're daft,' Lizzie said. 'Mum says she's taking us to the circus tomorrow, d'you want to come? It's a modern circus – you know, no tigers or things. Only the flying trapeze. People getting zapped instead of animals.'

'Are there any horses?'

'Might be. I don't think horses count.'

Rowan didn't see the point of a circus without horses.

'Ma says we're all too serious. Not me. Just the others. Charlie's in a great gloom because of losing time with his collarbone and Mr Hicks was on the phone and Mum took the phone off Charlie and told him – Mr Hicks – to shut up – not exactly shut up but in a polite sort of way, you know. But quite fierce. "We're not bowing and scraping to him just because he owns that horse!" she said – quite put out, for her. Then Charlie said we'd all starve without Mr Hicks and they had a row, so then Ma said we'd all go to the circus, just like that. She told us to ask Matty too. We said only if not her mother too, and that's arranged. But we don't mind your mother if she wants to come.'

Rowan supposed it would be quite fun, all of them. She and her mother never went anywhere new but, with High Hawes up the road, she never wanted anywhere else. They went in two cars, the two mothers driving, and Lizzie and Shrimp and Matty came with Rowan and her mother. As they sat squashed in the back, following the Haweses' Land-Rover up over the long hill out of the village, Matty said to Rowan, 'I hear you went round Sparrow Farm on Birdie and jumped the water?'

'Not the top one. Only the middle.'

'Were you surprised?' Shrimp asked Matty. 'We were, when we heard.'

'You *are* rude, Shrimp!' Lizzie snapped. 'You're not supposed to say things like that.'

'Well, it's true. Josephine said, after Swallow, she thought Rowan'd never get it together. And now she has. That's not rude.'

'It's Birdie,' said Rowan. 'Not me.'

'It must be a bit you,' Matty said.

'Oh, Rowan always thinks she's no good,' Lizzie said.

'She was right once,' Shrimp said. 'But not now,' she added hastily.

'Has your ma said anything about you riding again?' Lizzie asked Matty.

'Oh, yes, she's forever talking about it. I don't say anything. She's looked at a couple of ponies but I refused to go. She says it'll do me good. Take me out of myself, she says. But I say, look what it did in the first place. I wouldn't need taking out of myself if I hadn't been half-killed already.'

Rowan's heart sank into her best shoes. Mrs Prebble was looking now! And Matty didn't want one anyway.

'Isn't there any sort of pony you'd like?' she asked desperately.

'I wouldn't mind one – the sort that doesn't exist!' Matty laughed. 'Like a car. You know. Turn the key and it starts. Put the brake on and it stops.'

Rowan felt her evening was ruined at the turn the conversation had taken. Mrs Prebble was looking already! It was only July and there were still two months to go before her lease on Birdie was up.

When they got to the circus car-park Mrs Hawes said it looked like a hospital outing, with Matty on her crutches and Charlie with his arm in a sling, and they all got the giggles. Shrimp tied a white scarf round her head like a bandage and Hugh affected a worse limp than Matty's. Rowan tried to pretend it was all very funny but she was so cast down by Matty's remarks that she couldn't join in. It was pretty feeble anyway; she bit her lip and hung back.

There were horses, thank goodness, she noticed.

A poster showed an Appaloosa (a spotted horse) standing on its hindlegs with a bespangled ring-mistress brandishing a whip. The same lady appeared to be selling the tickets, with her spangles on underneath a tracksuit – 'You can see,' Hugh remarked. 'In circuses, they all do everything.'

In spite of the several local councils who wouldn't have the circus on their land, the show seemed to be attracting a good crowd on the hot summer evening. Even Rowan forgot her woes when the clowns came on and the canned music started blaring. There were no tigers or elephants, but a very funny goat which butted the clowns, four poodles, a horse just like the Armchair that cantered round and round for a couple of acrobats to leap on and off, and a troop of six Shetlands which did a display, circling, rearing, and bowing to the crowd. Hugh said he bet he could teach Cascade to do a few things like that and Shrimp said Cascade reared and bucked already, what was so special? And Hugh said, 'You could sell them Bonzo. Just what he's fit for,' so Shrimp hit him and Joan Hawes had to call them to order.

Near the end, before the flying trapeze, the bespangled lady brought on two liberty horses, a matching pair of Appaloosas, and they did a high-school act. At one point one of them lay down and she got on its back. It then got up and she twirled about a bit before jumping off.

Lizzie said to Matty, 'That's what you want, one that'll lie down for you to get on.'

Matty laughed. 'My mother would die – all those spots!'

The idea slipped into Rowan's head, hearing the exchange – a circus horse! They seemed to do it by word of mouth. No legs to make them go: they were totally obedient to the lady in spangles. She twirled her whip and pointed with it, but never touched them. She spoke to them a lot, quite quietly, and gave them something when they had reared up and walked a few steps on their hindlegs. They watched her all the time and seemed to be very attached to her. They were in beautiful condition, with shining coats.

'I'm sure I could do that,' Hugh said when they went out.

'You'd look lovely in spangles,' Lizzie jeered.

'Your legs in tights! They'd all pay to come and look!' Shrimp said.

After the flying trapeze act Charlie said, 'Think you could do that too, Hugh?' and Hugh grinned rather sheepishly and shook his head. At last, they all thought, something he couldn't do!

When Rowan got home her mother remarked

that she seemed a bit glum and Rowan told her why.

'I can't bear to lose Birdie! Not now!'

'I thought you were going to do some part exchange—?'

'Oh, Mum, I've got to find it first! I was thinking tonight, when that horse lay down, a circus horse might be just the thing. Save they're all spotted or piebald – Mrs Prebble hates coloured horses. You'd think, circus horses must retire after a bit, and need a good home – the Prebbles would be a very good home . . . but it's got to be a decent colour . . . how can I find out? That circus didn't have an address – I looked on their posters, but there was nothing. I suppose they are always travelling on.'

'They have winter quarters, I think.'

'If I could talk to that lady – she might help—'

'Surely if it was the right horse, Mrs Prebble wouldn't mind a funny colour?'

'No-one in their right mind would, but Mrs Prebble—!'

'Yes, she's not very understanding, is she? I could try and find out for you, if you like – go and talk to that circus woman. What do I have to ask for?'

'Oh, Mum – tell her what it's for: Matty having

a useless leg, and not even wanting to – it's got to be a kind, darling horse, and beautiful to suit Mrs Prebble, and darling for Matty to want it – and cheap, cheap enough so that we can afford it, to give to Mrs Prebble in exchange—'

'Part exchange, I thought you said.'

'Oh, *Mum*!' Rowan wailed.

'Oh, stop being neurotic, you're as bad as Mrs Prebble herself!' her mother said briskly. 'If we were to find this paragon of a horse, the thing to do would be send Mrs Prebble to see it, surely? Not buy it ourselves.'

'Yes!'

'And Matty too, I dare say. From what I've heard, she has more idea of what she wants than her mother does.'

'Yes, take Matty to see it! Not Mrs Prebble at all. Then she can tell her mother she wants it!'

Rowan's mother laughed. 'She might do it for you, Rowan, if you ask her nicely. She seems quite a sensible girl, not a bit like her mother.'

'Oh, Mum, yes!'

Rowan could see the idea taking shape. It only needed the right horse.

'When you're at school tomorrow I'll go and find that woman then, and ask questions. It's worth a chance. But don't bank on it, darling. I really think you're getting a bit obsessed with this pony business – it's not the whole world, you know.'

'Oh, but it is!' Rowan wanted to shout out. But she bit her tongue and kept the words to herself.

CHAPTER EIGHT

The team for the Barnfield Hill competition had to consist of four riders under fourteen. Auntie Millie chose Hugh and Rowan and two formidable sisters called Harriet and Fiona Brown. Harriet and Fiona rode a pair of ugly home-bred full-brothers called Bill Flowerpot and Ben Flowerpot. Both were good jumpers. None of them was brilliant at dressage and Josephine gave them some schooling in the test. Bill and Ben powered round the manège, lifting up their knees and tucking in their heads, and finished the test in half the time it should have taken; Hugh kept forgetting the way, and Rowan could never quite make out whether Birdie was on the right leg or not without looking down which Josephine told her was bad.

'I just hope you can all jump better than you can canter a circle,' she despaired.

Rowan had never jumped in a team competition before and discovered that it was much more harrowing than competing for oneself. If she made a hash of it, she would let the others down. They were supposed to be sporting and nice to each other in adversity, but Rowan couldn't see Hugh being nice to her if she boobed and stopped them winning.

'It's character-building,' Charlie said happily. 'If, for example, you fall off and break your collarbone, you smile and jump back on and finish the course because if you withdraw your team will be eliminated.'

Rowan wasn't too sure if he was joking or not. But it did seem rather like it. Josephine said it wasn't as bad as that these days because now when you fell off they made you lie still until they decided you weren't fatally injured, which sometimes took ages – 'Not like when we were little; Auntie Millie would push you back in the saddle and clap your pony on the backside before you knew what had happened. But, in a team, you do feel dreadful if you let the others down, it's quite true.'

None of this inspired Rowan with confidence.

Josephine said, 'Just get it in perspective, Rowan. It's only a fun thing, when all's said and done. *Enjoy* it! Charlie's not saying anything, but when he rides Out of the West in his first proper event in September, if he doesn't do well it could mean we're all out of a living here! Mr Hicks is such an impatient man, and doesn't really understand the business at all. It makes it so difficult. Think of all that when you worry about Birdie.'

'Oh, I will! I'm sorry!'

'Don't expect to win or anything. Just do your best and remember it's fun!'

'Yes!'

The worse she did, of course, the better it would be for selling Birdie – no-one would want her. Rowan tried to remember this.

Her mother hadn't got very far with the circus lady. When she went to find her, she discovered the circus had moved on, and nobody seemed to know where to. She found out its itinerary eventually by contacting a theatre ticket agency, and drove to one of its most convenient sites, which even then was fifty miles away. The circus lady hadn't got any old horses but gave her the name of a farm in Surrey where she thought a retired acrobat had a few 'resting' horses. She wasn't sure if she remembered the man's name correctly, and the address had no telephone number that she knew of.

'We can't get in touch without a name, not without actually going there, can we?'

'We can go there! On Sunday!'

Pauline Watkins was dubious. 'I suppose it's not too far . . . the motorway . . . I'm sure it's a wild-goose chase, but—'

'Oh, please!'

They went. It was very hot and there was a tail-back on the motorway, and they couldn't find the village and Pauline Watkins was nervous about what on earth they were going to say when they got there . . . if they ever got there . . .

'I'll do the saying,' Rowan said firmly.

When they eventually found the farm they were somewhat alarmed to see that it was a very smart and beautiful place obviously owned by a Surrey stockbroker. They drove up a long avenue to an elegant house set about with manicured lawns and rose-beds. In a field beside the avenue some horses were grazing, but none of them looked like circus horses, more like hunters and children's ponies.

'You go and ask. They're probably all having sherry before lunch.'

Pauline parked beside several smart estate cars and a Rolls-Royce.

Rowan got out and knocked at the front door. A manservant answered and looked at her kindly. Rowan scrambled out her bit of paper from the circus lady.

'I'm looking for Mr – Mr—' The name was impossible to pronounce so she shoved the paper under the man's nose. 'We were given this address.'

The man took it.

'Oh, yes, Bob. He's round the back, dear. In a caravan. That way.' He pointed across the expanse of gravel which wound away behind a treble-doored garage.

Rowan thanked him and rushed back to the car. They drove round the garage and followed the gravel into a stable yard. At the back of the yard was a five-barred gate into a field, and at the gate stood two chestnut Arabs with long flaxen manes.

'They look like circus horses!'

The caravan, lodged beside a hay-barn, had diamond-glitter embellishments and windows with flowers engraved on them but it had a forlorn air in its retirement, and flat tyres. Its travelling days were over, as – it appeared – were Bob's. Bob was elderly, lame and garrulous. He offered them a cup of tea and told them the story of his life before they got around to the object of the visit. He was – had been – an acrobat before he fell fifty feet and missed the safety net . . . yes, the two chestnuts were retired liberty horses.

'Never been separated in their lives. And never will be, m'dear.'

Rowan knew Mrs Prebble hated Arabs and they certainly didn't want two. She put her case as clearly as possible. Retired, gentle, obedient . . . fantastic home . . . no spots . . .

'Mostly we put 'em down when they can't work no longer. It's kinder.'

'There must be one somewhere!'

'There ain't nothing here, m'dear.'

As Rowan looked about to burst into tears, Bob had a rapid rethink and said, 'There's an address as I can give you – woman who has Andalusians. The circus had a few off her; they're very easy to train. No spots. Very kind. Very nice horses. She always said she'd want 'em back if we finished with 'em. Particular sort of lady.'

Rowan had never heard of Andalusians, but took the address eagerly. It was in Norfolk, miles away. Pauline Watkins thanked the old man and they departed.

'I suppose you want me to drive to Norfolk now?'

'We could ring her.'

'Ask her for a free horse, on the phone?'

'Oh, Mum!'

Rowan was in despair again. Her mother got cross and told her to stop wanting the impossible and they had a row. A bad day, Rowan thought gloomily – all because of her good intentions. She asked Josephine what an Andalusian was.

'Very old Spanish breed, very nice horse. It's not a breed that's taken off in England, not in a big way. Not tall enough perhaps, or overshadowed by the Arab.'

'How big?'

'Fifteen two-ish.'

Later Rowan looked it up in a book and it said, '. . . It has enormous presence and an appearance of great elegance . . . though courageous and spirited, few breeds are more docile and gentle.' The very thing!

Her mother refused to go to Norfolk. 'It's a wild-goose chase, Rowan,' she said severely.

Rowan daren't ask Charlie, and didn't want to talk to Lizzie about it in case Hugh got to know. It was such a long shot and her mother had lost patience, so she knew she was being a bit stupid about the whole thing.

'Once you get an idea into your head, you can't leave it alone,' her mother said crossly. 'You're like a dog with an old bone. You bury it somewhere and then keep going back to it. You can't arrange other people's lives, Rowan, you should know that by now.'

'It's mine I'm trying to arrange.'

'Well, it seems to involve a lot of other people.'

Her mother refused to ring up the woman in Norfolk, so Rowan decided she would ring the woman herself. She had to wait till her mother was out, and then she dithered for half an hour before she dared dial the number. Even she could see it was a bit of a cheek to ask a perfect stranger for a free, or very cheap horse. Perhaps she could—

'Arbuthnot speaking.' The voice was like a bark. Rowan jumped.

'Um—'

'Who's that? Speak up!'

Rowan was so frightened she put the phone down. Then she cried. She wanted to ring back but didn't dare. Then she cried because she was so *feeble*. She couldn't just leave it now. The sense of failure would be too awful. In the end she wrote down what she wanted to say on a piece of paper and held it in front of her as she dialled the Norfolk number. It trembled in her hand so she could scarcely see what she had written.

'Arbuthnot speaking!'

'I understand you have Andalusian horses?' She tried to sound like Mrs Prebble, tough and confident.

'Yes.' Another bark.

'I am looking for a retired Andalusian horse to go to an excellent home to be ridden by a girl who was severely injured in a riding accident. She wants a suitable horse to get rehabilitated.' (The last sentence didn't sound so good said as it looked written down, and she stumbled over rehabilitated – six syllables!) She pressed on, 'It needs to be perfectly quiet but willing and good-looking and preferably bay.' Her voice got progressively less like Mrs Prebble's and more like Rowan Watkins's with every word.

'You don't want much, do you? Who are you?'

'I'm Rowan Watkins.' With a burst of inspiration (not written down) she added, 'Bob somebody gave me your address. He's an old circus man in Surrey, an acrobat – he fell off – he has two retired Arabs and he told me about you. He said to go and see you, but you're rather far away.'

'Are you a child?' asked Ms Arbuthnot suspiciously.

'I'm just twelve.'

'The horse is for you?'

'No, my friend. She's fourteen, and a very good

rider, but her legs don't work now, so we thought – perhaps – a retired circus horse, that does things if you tell it . . .' Rowan, listening to herself, had never heard such a load of rubbish. She added valiantly, 'It's a very experienced home. Her mother's a Pony Club instructor.'

'Why isn't her mother ringing me up then?'

Rowan groaned. It would take all night to explain.

There was a long silence.

Then, 'Listen, child. I have a horse that might suit you, a pensioned off *haute école* horse, not old, but with some hindleg trouble that means he can't perform any more. I would let him go for nothing to a very good home, for hacking. But you would have to come and see me and I would have to come and see the home and all sorts of things like that which I think an adult would have to arrange. So if you are still interested sort it out with some responsible person and call me back.'

With which she put the phone down.

Rowan sat stunned. Having expected nothing, in seconds she had cracked the whole conundrum. She found it hard to believe, and was even tremblier now than when she started. She lay back in the armchair, staring at the cracked ceiling, taking long, calming breaths. The ceiling whirled. The magic horse existed! What next?

What next seemed to be team practice for the competition – nobody wanted to know about Rowan's circus horse.

'Count me out,' said Charlie. 'I've told you – I won't do another deal with Mrs P for all the tea in China.'

Josephine, rather more reluctantly, agreed. 'We can do nothing right for that woman. We really can't get involved with her again, Rowan. Anything we find for Matty is bound to be wrong.'

Pauline Watkins said it was no good going all that way with Rowan – neither of them knew enough about horses.

'Just tell Mrs Prebble you've found her a horse. Won't that do?'

'She won't take it from me! She'd take it from Charlie or Josephine, but not me. Especially if she knows it's a circus horse. She's a terrible snob about horses.'

'Well, honestly, Rowan, you do get crazy ideas. It seems you want you and me to go to Norfolk and bring back this horse on the offchance Mrs Prebble might find it suitable for Matty. Just a chance! For goodness' sake tell Mrs Prebble what you've found and leave it to her. Or tell Matty. It's for Matty, after all.'

But Rowan knew Mrs Prebble wouldn't go all the way to Norfolk to look at a horse that she, Rowan, recommended. If she took Matty and Matty liked it, she might persuade her mother. But how could they get there? Worrying about the Andalusian horse made Rowan almost forget the competition, so that when there was a last dressage practice at High Hawes with Josephine in charge and Auntie Millie turned up to give them a sort of before Agincourt lecture she had to bring her mind back to the problem in hand – which suddenly seemed a larger problem than Matty's horse. Auntie Millie took her on one side.

'I'm rather throwing you in at the deep end, Rowan. Just do your best, that's all I'm asking. It will be splendid practice for you to ride in this sort of competition.'

Rowan recognized this as a sort of let-out if she did badly, and as a sign that great things were not expected of her. Instead of comforting her, it spiked her pride. Auntie Millie hadn't seen her giving Out of the West a lead over the water! She glowered.

'Why, you look just like Hugh!' Auntie Millie said, and laughed. She had a laugh like a hyena. She patted Rowan on the knee and said, 'You're my girl, Rowan!' and wandered off.

What this meant, Rowan had no idea.

The day of the Barnfield competition was the same day as Charlie had to take Out of the West to his first big event. Josephine was going with him and Priscilla was going to ride Wilfred in the Novice competition. They commandeered the big horse-box and left the trailer for Hugh and Rowan. Joan Hawes was going to drive the ponies.

'I'm really sorry I can't come with you,' Josephine said to Rowan. 'You're on your own today, but just remember, keep cool, think of it as good practice, not something you've got to win. Just do your own thing, enjoy it!'

Is that what she was going to say to Charlie, Rowan wondered? Charlie seemed to be giving Hugh a big talking-to, very stern, and Hugh was looking wriggly and cross, but afterwards Charlie came across to Rowan and said, 'Good luck, Rowan.'

'And you!'

If only she could go with him and watch him on Out of the West! She knew it would be spectacular and that, in his way, he was as nervous as she was, because of Mr Hicks. If Out of the West had been his own horse . . . But if he had been, she knew he wouldn't be going. Charlie thought it was too soon. His shoulder still hurt him because he hadn't rested it enough, and he looked drawn and serious.

After they had departed, Rowan and Hugh loaded their ponies into the trailer and Lizzie and Shrimp came out with a huge picnic basket. Mrs Prebble called in to drop Matty, who wanted to travel with them in the Land-Rover instead of with her mother, and Mrs Prebble said to Rowan, 'Don't let the pony down, my girl.'

Lizzie, overhearing, put her tongue out and as Mrs Prebble flounced round she saw her. Lizzie, very quickly, said to Rowan, 'I've got an ulcer on my tongue. Can you see it?'

They then got the giggles, and Lizzie kept saying, 'Don't let the pony down, my girl!' in her Mrs Prebble voice, and Hugh was let in on the joke and joined in. They then noticed that Matty was looking horribly miserable and stopped, because she had to live with the woman, poor girl.

'She can't help it,' Matty said miserably.

'Come on, squash up,' Joan Hawes said cheerfully, to change the subject. 'Give Matty some room, Hugh. Or get in the front with me – that would be best.'

They checked that they hadn't forgotten anything. It was going to be tough without Josephine or Charlie to mastermind them – even Hugh was used to having their back-up. But when they got on the road Rowan found that her excitement rather over-rode everything else, and little fountains of fear and joy and terror and anticipation kept bursting up in turns in her inner regions. Surely she was practised enough now to take it all more calmly? But being in a team was different. It mattered terribly, doing well.

The Barnfield Hill event was set in old-fashioned farmland, with hedges. There was a huge field to collect in, edged on one side by a large wood. A jump ominously called the Leaf Slide led into the wood, and down a winding path to a coffin jump over a track, then up and out into a big park where there was a long uphill gallop with fallen trees to jump. On the way back, downhill, there were some island jumps, then some rails back into the wood and another winding path leading steeply down to a stream which one had to jump across banks strengthened with railway sleepers.

'Lots of 'em refuse here,' Hugh said casually, as they walked around.

Lizzie said, being Josephine, 'You've got to get her back well in control, coming home into the wood, Rowan, because the long gallop through the park makes them all tizzed up. If you come too fast down to the stream you'll hit a tree, or miss the right line to the jump.'

'And lots of spectators stand there to watch the fun,' Hugh said, 'and they get in the way.'

'No, they don't,' Lizzie said. 'Not if the fence judge is any good. But Birdie might be spooked by them. She's not done much of this before.' Then, seeing Rowan's look, she added soothingly, 'But she'll be heading for home and loving it, don't worry.' Then she couldn't help adding, 'But don't come too fast!'

Rowan missed Josephine, who would have walked the course with her sternly and helpfully. Hugh had done the course several times before and threw out what he thought was useful information, but in a really scaring way. Rowan knew that it was harder for her, on a pony strange to the course. The Flowerpots had both ridden the course before, too. She would be the discard, she was convinced. (Only the best three in the team of four were counted for the results.) But Fiona Flowerpot said, 'Don't be bothered – it's nice. I bet your dressage is better than Hugh's.'

Rowan didn't think so, as she had seen Hugh really trying at home, and he was good. Anyway,

Hugh was on her side. It wasn't Hugh she had to beat, but her erstwhile Swallow, who was in the home team. He was being unboxed across the field by Tom Thug, and Rowan went to see him. Tom Thug let her hold him while he fetched his tack. Swallow nuzzled her in a friendly way and Rowan was sure he remembered her. He looked very well and fit, and Rowan was comforted by the fact that he was doing what he wanted to do with his proper owner, not having to go slowly like he had with her.

'You were too clever for me, Swallow,' Rowan whispered.

She gave him a Polo mint and he licked her hand. He had old sores at the corners of his mouth, she noticed, from his severe bit. But he had only himself to blame, as Hugh would have said. She walked back to Birdie, confused with her allegiances.

Auntie Millie arrived and boomed encouragement at them. Although she said things about enjoying it and just doing your best and made out it was fun, Rowan thought that in her heart Auntie Millie was as keen on winning as Mrs Prebble. She had a sort of glint in her eye. She hadn't really ridden in all those point-to-points just for fun, Rowan guessed. Her house was said to be full of tarnished silver cups from the glory days of her past.

They had to ride the dressage test first, then go cross-country, and show-jump last. It helped a lot with one's score to do a good dressage test, and Rowan had practised diligently with Josephine and hoped to get off to a good start. Birdie was the right shape for it and was naturally balanced, which was a great help. Bill and Ben the Flowerpot Men powered round as usual, fast but accurate, with their noses tucked in and their large hooves hammering out perfect circles. They were Welsh cobs, and almost indistinguishable, bright bays with heavy black tails. Of their team, Birdie was the only elegant member but, as Auntie Millie was fond of saying, handsome is as handsome does.

Hugh went in and Rowan stood waiting, her heart beginning to pound uncomfortably. Lizzie stood by her in her Josephine role, and they watched Hugh get halfway through the test then forget what came next. Luckily he was quite near them and Lizzie saw him pull up and shouted at him quickly, 'Change rein at K, sitting trot!' The judge, about to give him the hooter, desisted.

'Idiot,' Lizzie said.

His free walk turned into a trot and his canter circles were wild, and Rowan thought with a certain satisfaction that she might, if she was lucky, get a better score than Cascade.

It was the first test she had ever attempted in proper competition. Hugh had thought he could do it standing on his head, but Rowan's intense, nervous concentration made Birdie prick up her ears and gather herself together in her best Josephine-drilled manner, wondering what the tension was for. She bent her long neck softly to the bit and streamers of foam flew from her mouth as she circled elegantly on the proper leg, to left and to right. Rowan remembered not to look down, not quite sure if she was on the proper leg save that it felt like it, and Lizzie would have hissed at her if she wasn't – she was close enough. Hugh sat watching, scowling. Birdie felt pliable and sweet as a willow twig in the breeze: Rowan could not believe her luck. She pulled her back for the free walk . . . a bit too free . . . Birdie looked up, saw Cascade and whinnied – horrors! Rowan gave her a sharp kick and she gave a prance and a skitter, then relaxed again. About two out of ten for free walk, Rowan thought crossly. All Hugh's fault! After that not much went wrong, apart from not making her transitions in quite the right places, and the usual trouble with standing square for the halt – squarish, but not perfect. And Birdie bit at a fly on her leg before moving off.

'That was good!' Lizzie said.

'Well done, my gel!' said Auntie Millie. 'You seem to get on well with that pony. Better than that little hellcat Hugh had at camp last year. I thought that was yours?'

'It's Tom Thug's now. Tom Trugg, I mean.'

'Hotspur? Is that the same pony?'

'Yes.'

'Well, blow me. We had it in camp and I never recognized it!'

They stayed to watch Swallow/Hotspur do his dressage test, for which Rowan didn't envy Tom Thug. The pony, knowing that the day was for jumping, was in his most excitable mood, and put in several bucks when cantering. How Tom Thug managed to get him to walk at all Rowan found incredible, and standing still after the halt . . . the pony sort of bounced on the spot, every muscle quivering with the effort of restraining himself.

'Damned good riding, to get any sort of a score on that animal,' Auntie Millie exclaimed.

'He'll make up for it the rest of the day though,' Matty said.

She was bounding about on her crutches, not noticeably upset not to be competing. The grass was too rough for her wheelchair. Rowan thought of the perfect, gentle horse . . . but no, not to worry about that now! The cross-country was already under way and her number was coming up fast.

Now she felt the panics rising.

Lizzie, seeing her face, said, 'Don't be daft. Birdie will fly over everything.' She put her arms round Birdie's neck and laid her cheek against the gleaming coat. 'I wonder how Charlie's doing?'

Rowan thought of Charlie's strained face, and thought of Mr Hicks watching him, his tight, money-maker's lips pursed up. If Prissy made a hash of it on Wilfred, her father would be in a terrible mood. Charlie had to bear the brunt of it, for both Prissy and himself, and mustn't answer back. It made her feel a lot better, that her day was quite simple compared with Charlie's.

The first teams were already on the cross-country course and messages came back that nobody was going clear so far. The water was causing trouble as usual and a jump in the park near the pond, where one approached round quite a sharp bend under trees, was getting quite a lot of run-outs. Mrs Prebble was out scouting for them and sent a message back: 'Approach it at a trot!'

'Yes*sir*!' said Hugh crossly. 'What an old bosscat your mother is,' he said to Matty. But Matty only laughed. She seemed to enjoy not doing it, only watching. But Rowan thought what a waste it was, when she was such a brilliant rider. Life was very unfair.

Matty said, 'I'm going out to the wood to watch you go round. You can see more from the edge. Are you coming, Lizzie?'

'All right.'

Lizzie wasn't sure if it was fair to leave Rowan before the off, but she had Hugh and Harriet and Fiona with her, so she set off with the swinging Matty. Someone in a car quite soon gave them a lift, Rowan was pleased to see. Matty was a real goer on her crutches, just like on her ponies. Without Lizzie, she got the trembles again. But then Auntie Millie came over and made them all laugh. 'It's chaos out there. You've just got to go very steadily and *think*. The trouble is all being caused by witless riding. I know you will have no problems.' There was no reply to that.

They rode down to the collecting ring. As all their ponies were goers they were more concerned with keeping them calm than riding them in, so they walked round together in big circles. Tom Thug set off on Swallow, obviously without anyone having told him to approach the jumps at a trot. Watching him, Rowan was filled with relief at the way things had turned out – she could never have done that! Swallow flew into the wood, and came home in very short time, the first clear.

'No-one will beat Hotspur,' Rowan heard someone say.

Tom Thug got off and loosened his girths and, still on his feet, walked Swallow round to cool him off. It was apparent now that he was getting rather large for the pony, and was resting him as much as possible. Hugh watched him thoughtfully. Hugh was quite small for his age, much lighter than Tom Thug.

Hugh was going to go first, then Harriet on Bill Flowerpot, Fiona on Ben and Rowan last. Hugh set off fast, but did not appear again for a long time, and Harriet was not allowed to go as the All Clear signal did not come from the wood.

'Something's gone wrong,' Harriet said. 'It must be a fall, to be so long.'

'That means Hugh will be our discard score,' Fiona said. 'His dressage was pretty dire as well.'

Rowan listened to these seasoned campaigners making their calm assessments, and realized that if Hugh's was the discard score, hers was going to have to count. Not only did this thought scare her rigid, but she seemed to be the only one wondering if Hugh or Cascade were hurt. Harriet and Fiona were only thinking about winning.

But soon Harriet was given the flag to go, and Hugh appeared again jumping out of the wood, with Lizzie running some way behind and Matty hopping in their wake. Cascade's white front was caked with mud, and Hugh had twigs in his collar and blood trickling out of his nose.

'What happened?' Fiona squeaked.

'He slipped going into the water – completely lost his legs and hit the sleepers. We all went flying. I landed right up the far side and hit the tree, and he got wedged in the ditch and we had a devil of a job to get him out. I hope he's all right.'

He slipped off, undid the girths and started to examine Cascade's legs.

Rowan thought he did seem to get into a lot of trouble, in spite of being such a good rider – no doubt Auntie Millie's exhortations to trot had fallen on deaf ears. Perhaps someone like herself, only too anxious to trot instead of gallop, might do better? It then occurred to her that she had to, if Hugh was now their discard member. A fall was sixty faults. That gave her several refusals in hand (twenty faults for first, forty for second) before she topped his score. Awful butterflies started to dance in her stomach. If Hugh couldn't jump the water . . .

'Oh, Hugh! Poor Cascade! Is he all right?'

Lizzie came running up, and Auntie Millie appeared in a Land-Rover shouting, 'You idiot boy! Too fast! Too fast!'

'I couldn't help it. I couldn't stop him.'

'Pony all right?'

Rowan decided the excitement was not doing Birdie any good and rode away from them trying not to think disaster. Harriet came back in one piece but said she had had a stop, and Fiona cantered off with her jaw set looking like Winston Churchill. Rowan rode down to the start and they all shouted Good Luck at her, and the starter took her number.

'Twenty seconds.'

Rowan trotted two small circles and the starter shouted, 'Off you go!' and set the stop-watch. Rowan was cantering without being aware of having done anything to tell Birdie – Birdie was obviously delighted to be away, and was taking a strong hold and the Leaf Slide was coming up fast. This was one of the trot-at jumps, because it had a drop that the pony didn't see until the last minute, and if it was going fast and put the brakes on suddenly one was bound to jump it alone. Or so

Rowan thought. She slowed down, Birdie boggled, stopped, and jumped. Rowan shot up in the air and bit her tongue but landed back in the right place on the way down. Slither and snort . . . Birdie scrambled clear, shook her head, and trotted fast along the winding path – not a fast place, as it twisted so. She was all eyes to see what was coming next.

Rowan saw a knot of spectators and a jump judge sitting on a shooting-stick looking expectantly her way. The jump was over a telegraph pole into a slightly sunken lane, two strides across and up the other side. Josephine would have been shouting, 'Legs!' Rowan thought, so she drove on as she felt Birdie looking at everything except the jump. She came to the bar, boggled again and did the same cat-hop over as she had done at the Leaf Slide. But clear. She leapt out with great enthusiasm and tore away up the wide ride on the other side to the jump that led out of the wood. Horses always jumped well out of a wood, out into the open away from imagined lions and tigers. Birdie flew it and went tearing out into the park with her glorious long thoroughbred stride. This is where the going-steady advice got thrown to the winds and the ponies got into their galloping mode, loving the great open expanse ahead of them and the excitement of the jumps. Rowan began to understand only too well why there had been disasters out here, for the going-slow advice was almost impossible to heed. And going fast was gorgeous! She felt like singing as they flew a fallen log so fast it hardly felt like a jump, just a longer stride. How she trusted Birdie! She would never have done this on Swallow, just been simply bolted with and scared stiff. But when she took a pull at Birdie, at the top of the hill, Birdie dropped her head and came back to her. Just as well, for she remembered that the next jump was the one causing trouble. There was a pond in the middle of the park with trees round it, and one had to ride round the pond, between markers, ducking under the trees, and jump a sort of garden seat with straw bales sitting in it which one couldn't see until the last minute because of the trees.

'Trot,' Rowan remembered, and trotted. No wonder most ponies had run out! Even scrupulously doing what she was told, Rowan came to the seat very suddenly. Birdie stopped with a jolt, but at least it was from a trot and not a fast canter and Rowan didn't go flying over her head. She sat down hard, kicked like crazy and Birdie leapt forward, clearing it in one enormous bound. Miraculously, Rowan stayed with her and they belted down the long hill. There was a jump of heavy poles in the way which they took in their stride – good steering, Rowan congratulated herself! – then it was panic stations: the jump back into the wood coming up fast and darkness beyond.

However had Tom Thug managed to stop Swallow here, Rowan wondered? She came on it too fast and jumped it luckily. Birdie skewed and her back legs rattled on the top. Rowan lost her seat and a stirrup and hauled on the reins in a sweat. The path ahead was twisting and steeply downhill and no place to be going fast. Birdie came almost to a halt, rather cross, and Rowan got her stirrup and her breath back.

Clear so far! Now the nasty water-jump where Cascade had come to grief. The path twisted steeply down between the trees, and Birdie slithered on her hocks, following the gruesome score marks of those that had gone before. The ditch yawned black below. It wasn't big, but looked formidable in the dark shadow of the trees. Rowan felt Birdie quail beneath her. Don't stop now! – twenty faults they couldn't afford! Spectators crowded the far bank, tucked back into the undergrowth. How they must have enjoyed poor Cascade getting stuck and Hugh flying through the air, Rowan thought angrily, and gave Birdie such a determined clap with her legs that the mare stopped boggling and hopped over it with an air of amazement.

After that it was uphill to a lovely jump out into the field and back to the finish over a water trough which Birdie jumped with about a metre to spare.

'Well done!' Auntie Millie was shouting as Rowan pulled up.

'I went clear!' Rowan squeaked.

'Fantastic!'

'Wonderful! Fiona went clear too, so we're in with a chance.'

Auntie Millie's eyes gleamed and the hairs on her chin bristled with triumph. Hugh stood scowling, not a good loser.

'It will all depend on the show-jumping,' Auntie Millie said. 'We have two clears and a twenty for the cross-country, the same as Barnfield Hill. Our dressage scores are better than theirs – Swallow was a disaster there, but he'll go clear jumping, that's for sure. It won't be decided until the very end, by the look of it.'

Mrs Prebble came toiling up the hill with Matty swinging along beside her. She was beaming for once.

'Our little mare went very well,' she enthused.

Our, thought Rowan! The remark went over her like a douse of cold water. She wanted to shout, '*MY* little mare!' but was too cowardly.

'Rowan's riding got her round,' Auntie Millie said tartly.

Mrs Prebble did not reply, but her smug look did not disappear.

'There's great potential there.'

'As a pair,' said Auntie Millie. 'They understand each other. Birdie's not done well with anyone else.'

'She's young. Still learning,' said Mrs Prebble.

She still owned her, after all, and her enthusiasm was valid enough. Rowan, through a sudden blur of tears, saw Auntie Millie's lovely chin jutting aggressively, and thought – like a flash – 'Auntie Millie will sort out the circus horse for me!' Why ever hadn't she thought of it before? Of course Mrs Prebble would take Auntie Millie's word that the horse was the right horse – if it was, of course. Thrown by all these conflicting emotions, she slipped down from Birdie and laid her cheek against the sweaty neck, hiding her face. It *must* come right, she vowed.

She saw then how it was for Hugh, wanting Swallow and not getting him, and being so ambitious, and she was nice to him and he told her how he had made such a bad mistake at the ditch. He owned up to it, responding to her sympathy. He was worried about Cascade, having got stuck, and wondered whether he had strained anything. But there was no evidence of anything being wrong.

Their mothers opened up the picnic basket and they scoffed eagerly. Rowan's head was in a whirl. She found it hard to believe how well it had gone for her so far – failure had become so engrained. At last she saw, like everybody else, that losing Swallow had been a blessing in disguise.

Auntie Millie went to study the score sheets which were being pinned on the side of the Secretary's caravan. The fewest penalties, for dressage and cross-country, were scored by themselves and Barnfield Hill. They led Barnfield Hill by four marks.

'That's one knock-down in the show-jumping.' She shook her head. 'Very close.'

Rowan did not want to think about it. Doing what Josephine said, just going for a sensible ride, not thinking about winning, was going to be very hard. With her new idea about the circus horse, and horrible Mrs Prebble's threats, her head was whirling and beginning to ache. Lizzie told her to calm down.

'It's only a potty competition. As if it matters!'

It didn't, but seemed to, terribly. To make it worse, she saw Mrs Prebble talking to the man who had enquired whether Birdie was for sale at Otty's show. She turned away, sick with anxiety. The better she did, the more the man would offer!

The show-jumping had started and Auntie Millie took them off to walk the course. It was rider demanding, all twists and turns, but only two really formidable jumps, a double and a high set of upright rails. There was a time to get round in, but generous enough. It wasn't against the clock. The advice Auntie Millie was shouting out went right past Rowan's ears. She couldn't take any more of it. She knew she just had to go very carefully and not get lost. She studied the course plan and forgot about the actual jumps. Losing one's way was going to be very easy. Lizzie said she'd stand on the ropes and shout at her if she looked like going wrong. Hugh said she'd be eliminated for outside advice.

'I'll shout quietly,' Lizzie said.

'I won't go wrong,' Rowan said stonily.

She seemed to have no heart left. She felt drained and empty. Lizzie looked at her anxiously and said, 'I don't know why anybody does this. Hugh's as sick as a parrot and you look as if you're going to throw up any minute.'

'It's Mrs Prebble,' Rowan muttered.

'Oh, her – enough to make anyone throw up.' Then she added, 'Get on. It's better when you've started.'

Luckily their time to jump was after Barnfield Hill's, so they would know exactly how much effort was needed. The third-placed team was not much below them and they could blow it completely if things didn't go right for them. But so could the others. They circled the collecting ring, the four of them together. The Flowerpot Men were eager but not always accurate jumpers, Cascade would go clear but what good was that now he had made a cricket score in the cross-country? And Birdie . . . Birdie was as good as her rider, Rowan thought, quailing.

The first Barnfield Hill rider went in, the high-powered Melinda Bottomly. She was smooth and stony-faced and, although presumably only fourteen, looked seventeen and rode a fifteen-two horse.

'Her parents run a training centre for eventers,' Fiona Flowerpot said to Rowan. 'Not fair, is it?'

About to agree, it struck Rowan that, hopeless as she was, she was trained by fairly professional people herself. How could she say it wasn't fair? Melinda did a copybook round. She had gone clear in cross-country and had the lowest dressage score of the day.

'Yuk,' said Hugh.

Now that he was the discard score and didn't care, they all knew he would do a super clear. It just worked that way. Rowan thought if she knocked everything down and fell off or was eliminated, Hugh's score would count after all. The way she felt, she thought that was what would happen.

The next two Barnfield riders also went clear. The crowd cheered and clapped. Their boss lady was looking pleased, as well she might, with only brilliant Swallow to go.

'If he's clear, you've all got to go clear as well to win,' Auntie Millie said. 'No room for any knock-downs at all.'

They had worked that out already and didn't think it was possible.

Swallow, after cross-country, was a double handful for Tom Thug, prancing into the ring and crabwising to the first jump as his rider tried to contain him. Rowan heard someone say what a dangerous pony Hotspur was and shouldn't be allowed in the Pony Club but the person standing next to her said he was brilliant and brilliance was rare. 'A rider for that sort of brilliance is rarer,' said the critic, and Rowan could not quite believe that this was the pony she had tried to learn to ride on – no wonder she had felt in a permanent panic about the whole thing!

If Swallow was brilliant, so was Tom Thug, she realized, letting him go on and trusting the pony's own judgement, but turning him with rare skill round the tight turns. But as he came in to the nasty double he turned too quickly and got Swallow wrong. Swallow, unbalanced and off his stride, made a valiant leap over the first bar which stayed put, but then was all wrong for the second bar and was forced to refuse. It was patently a rider fault. Tom Thug's poker face remained stony. He turned back and jumped the obstacle perfectly and finished without fault, but that made Barnfield Hill seven faults down (three for a refusal).

It was terribly hard not to cheer at Swallow's mistake. It was magic luck for them, they all acknowledged what a clever rider Tom Thug was. Rowan could see from his thoughtful expression that Hugh was actually wondering if Tom Thug might ride better than he did. He was silent, and almost jumped when Auntie Millie bawled, 'You're in first, Hugh – wake up!'

As he rode into the ring she said to the girls, 'Two down and you've lost it, remember. By one point. One down we can allow. Or two refusals. No more.'

The mathematics fazed Rowan.

Hugh rode a perfect clear, a copybook round, and came out looking almost tearful. Auntie Millie said, 'Well done, Hugh! Beautifully ridden.' She patted his knee in her grandmotherly fashion, knowing exactly how he felt – worse than ever to do so well after making such a hash of the cross-country. Her opposite number of the Barnfield Hill tribe, standing by the entrance to the ring, was white with tension. Rowan's mother was standing with Joan Hawes at the ringside – they were actually laughing and eating ice-creams! How could they? Rowan wondered, aghast. Already, although she was the last to go, her heart was hammering with nervousness. It was agony to watch the Flowerpot Men. They were eager and bold but rather clumsy and both rapped several jumps without actually dislodging anything. But just when they all felt it safe to let out their breath, Ben Flowerpot knocked the last jump hard. The pole leapt up in its cups, came down, bounced, and fell. A huge groan went up from the crowd. Rowan's heart went from hammering to plunging. She gathered up her reins.

Auntie Millie's chin bristled militantly. 'A clear,

Rowan,' she boomed, 'Or we're lost.'

They led by three points. One knock-down and they would lose by one. A refusal and it would be a tie. No-one wanted a tie.

'Birdie, save me!' Rowan whispered to her.

She no longer felt afraid of losing her way, having watched seven go round, and had learned a little from watching – certainly to get a good straight line at the tricky double. The rest was in the lap of the gods or, rather, in Birdie's dear heart. She would do everything in her power not to mess her up.

Birdie felt so lovely, keen but not silly. Just as she faced the first jump, Rowan thought of dear Charlie and Josephine, and all her stupid irresolution melted away. As if she had anything to be frightened of, when she had sailed over that water jump! They knew she could do it.

And I will, she said.

Birdie was no Swallow, fighting and plunging, but came to her hand every time she asked her to steady. Get her straight and right, and then legs and confidence, and over she flew. She was a natural jumper and needed only steering and her pace to be monitored. But Rowan knew that her seat was far less certain than Hugh's and Tom Thug's and Melinda Bottomly's – they had been riding all their lives and she only a year. It was much harder for her to land and be ready instantly to turn for the next jump which never seemed to be straight ahead, but always round a corner or skew on. Her heart was in her mouth, keeping her stirrups and her cool. She came to the double straight as planned, but Birdie jumped so big that the two strides in the middle were too short for her. She changed them into one and took off while Rowan was still landing – or so it felt to Rowan, flying through the air again before she was ready for it and getting left behind. She had the sense to let the reins slip, but then was tearing down on to the last jump with no control at all. She could sense the whole crowd holding its breath and Auntie Millie's anguish was as nothing to her own, seeing the round about to be blown apart at the very end.

But Birdie, galloping with joy, lifted and flew and the poles were miles below and Rowan was in heaven, hearing the great cheer that went up, carrying them on round the ring at forty miles an hour.

'Pull up, girl!' she heard the furious Barnfield lady shout, standing at the entrance to the ring, and Rowan pulled and Birdie saw that there was nothing left to jump and cantered politely out of the ring into the waiting arms of her fellows.

They were all shrieking with joy, but quietly, so

as not to be rude – squeaking more, eyes glittering with triumph.

'No-one can beat us now,' Auntie Millie said. 'Well done, my dear, that was a splendid round.'

Mrs Prebble came marching up, beaming again.

'Splendid!' she said to Birdie, and patted her neck. She did not look at Rowan.

Rowan slipped out of her saddle to loosen the girths, burying her head under the saddle-flap. She had to talk to Auntie Millie about the circus horse – there was no time to be lost. With every success Mrs Prebble's hold over Birdie was growing.

'Don't look so miserable – you're our heroine!' Auntie Millie was laughing. 'You've all done splendidly – and you too, Hugh – you can't win every time. Give the others a chance sometimes.'

She gave him an affectionate hug. How lucky they were to have such an encouraging boss; even if they had lost she would have encouraged them, Rowan knew, not like the awful Barnfield Hill lady who was spitting blood at the ringside and – no doubt – trying to work out if she could query the score in the cross-country to make a few more points. She only had to find four to win. She could still object.

Auntie Millie went off talking to Mrs Prebble

and Matty hopped up and stood looking quizzically at Birdie.

She said to Rowan, 'I really hated that mare. You've done wonders with her.'

Rowan said, 'It's not me. It's Josephine mostly.'

Hugh said, 'Your ma hypes them up too much, Charlie says.'

'Oh, Charlie says,' Matty repeated mockingly. 'We haven't all got a Charlie and Josephine, have we? Some of us have got a Mummy Prebble.' She laughed.

Rowan and Hugh didn't know how to take this remark. It was her own mother she was talking about.

'Well—' Hugh started, and then thought he shouldn't say it.

Rowan said, 'You could keep a horse with them, like me.'

'What horse?'

'The right one.'

'This myth,' said Matty.

'You do want—?' Rowan's voice shook.

Matty looked bleak suddenly. 'What's the use? I can't.'

'It's wanting that matters.' It mattered to Rowan, anyway.

'It's only days like now, watching you, makes

me think I – well – oh, don't talk about it! We don't talk about it, it's too embarrassing. Nobody does, haven't you noticed?'

Rowan thought it was true, what she said; they none of them asked Matty what it was like not being able to run about any more. They studiously avoided any talk of her disability, although they all thought about it quite a lot, and said poor Matty a lot to each other. To her, they pretended she was just the same as they were. It was a way of not getting embarrassed. It was perfectly obvious, on a day like this, that she would feel her loss keenly. She had been a brilliant rider, not just good. She had been in every Pony Club team going. Except with Birdie.

'Well, Ma's not going to leave the subject alone, that's for sure. Riding again. But she can't make me.'

They led their ponies back to the trailers. Rowan saw that the others thought the day was over, but she felt that for her it was only just starting.

CHAPTER NINE

Going home, Rowan asked Auntie Millie to give her a lift in her Land-Rover.

'I want to talk to you. It's very important.'

Looking at the white, set face, Auntie Millie could see it was.

'Very well, but I'll have to shift a few things first.'

The few things on the passenger seat turned out to be a bag of barley, a saddle needing stuffing, a box of eggs, an overflowing handbag and a bundle of binder twine. Rowan helped to stow it in the back, leaving the eggs and the handbag at her feet. Her mother and Joan Hawes made no comment and Rowan guessed they had asked Lizzie why, but Lizzie didn't know either. She appreciated being left alone. Interfering mothers were a pain.

'So what's this all about?'

The day was over, the prizes and rosettes had been distributed, the Barnfield Hill objection over-ruled. Horse-boxes and trailers were all trundling away over the field. Auntie Millie crashed her gears into first.

Rowan poured out her story, how her lease on Birdie was up in October and people wanted to buy her. But Mrs Prebble had *promised* – if they found the right horse for Matty . . . It went on and on, her story. The circus . . . the old acrobat . . . Mrs Arbuthnot . . .

'Amelia Arbuthnot, you mean? Our husbands used to shoot together. Funny old gel. You rang her up? How brave. Did she bark at you?'

'Yes. But she said . . .'

Rowan's spirits bounded at the thought of old Millie knowing Mrs Arbuthnot. But why not? Old horsy people knew each other, after all those years hunting and showing and breeding and milling around – it was natural. Encouraged, she rounded out her tale: 'She's got the right horse. But it's in Norfolk, and Charlie refuses to go and see it.'

She explained why.

'Well, I don't blame him. Lucy Prebble can be very difficult. But underneath, you know, if you dig deep down, she's not a bad stick. Thwarted in this life – same old story – makes her child do what she can't do herself. She was a brilliant show-jumper in her youth, as a child, you know. Quite famous. Very competitive.'

Auntie Millie overtook two horse-boxes, the ancient Land-Rover rattling so loudly that conversation was impossible for a while. When she slowed down again Rowan said, 'Would you go up to Norfolk and see if this horse is suitable for Matty? And if it is, tell Mrs Prebble that we've found the right horse?'

It was a terrible cheek, asking that. She countered, 'You could ring her first, perhaps, and ask about this horse. It's a pensioned-off *haute école* Andalusian.'

Auntie Millie didn't say anything. She passed a car and trailer, waving at the driver, and turned on to the road over the top of the downs that led to High Hawes.

Rowan remembered this was where Swallow, running loose, had caused Mrs Prebble to crash her car. It seemed a century ago! What was she doing, sitting in the famous Mrs Mildmay's car asking her to do this thing?

'Why not?' said Auntie Millie. 'I wouldn't mind seeing Amelia again.'

'You mean it?! And take me?'

'Yes, dear, why not? We can have a nice day out. Amelia knows a half-decent horse when she sees it. I'll have a chat with her on the phone.'

'Oh, yes, *please*! She said an adult. To talk to an adult.'

Rowan couldn't believe it. She wanted to throw her arms round Millie Mildmay and hug her, whiskers and all.

'Of course, it's crazy. To interfere, I mean. But it's true Lucy Prebble is still looking at show-jumpers for Matty. She's got tunnel vision. Quite unsuitable.'

'It can lie down, for her to mount,' Rowan breathed.

'How sweet! How nice. I'd like one like that. If Lucy turns it down, it might suit me.'

Rowan was now almost sobbing with joy. Why on earth couldn't she be cool? she wondered. Everything mattered so! She couldn't believe it when something went right for a change.

Millie Mildmay, very perceptive, said, 'Is it a secret, you finding this horse?'

'My mother knows and won't have anything to do with it. Nor will Charlie or Josephine. If we go, I'd rather they didn't know.'

'Fine. We'll keep it under our hat, eh? I'll ring Amelia tonight and have a chat.'

'Oh thank you!'

Rowan found that her day had turned into a red letter day with gold stars and cannons exploding. All her worries suddenly seemed over. And Birdie had been fabulous and so had she, not falling off or in any way making a fool of herself.

When Auntie Millie put her down and drove away the others had not yet arrived, but Charlie and Josephine were unboxing.

'How did you do?' Rowan shouted.

They laughed. They could see by her face that she had done very well.

'We won! We won!' she shouted. 'And Birdie was clear all the way, and show-jumping as well!'

They both hugged her, and said all the right things, and then told her that Wilfred had gone beautifully for Priscilla and they came fourth in the Novice and Mr Hicks was so pleased that he hadn't minded that Out of the West had done a bad dressage and knocked down three show-jumps – 'But he did a superb cross-country inside the time!' Mr Hicks had taken Priscilla home in glory and, before he departed, tipped Charlie ten pounds. 'Like I was a stable lad. I couldn't believe it!'

When the others came back they were all so excited that no-one thought to ask Rowan why she had travelled home with Auntie Millie. Even her mother never remarked on it, and when Auntie Millie rang later in the evening to talk to Rowan, she assumed it was to congratulate her on the day.

Mrs Mildmay told Rowan she had made an appointment for Sunday. 'Amelia has asked us both to lunch. How very nice! We'll have a good day out, however the horse turns out. I'll pick you up at ten o'clock, dear.'

Rowan didn't tell anyone, not even her mother, hugging the possibility to herself. Every day of the week seemed twice as long as usual. When Auntie Millie's old rattletrap pulled up outside their cottage on Sunday morning, Pauline Watkins was on top of a ladder upstairs decorating her bedroom. Rowan shouted up the stairs. 'I'll be back this evening!'

And the journey was under way, the battered Land-Rover tearing across the countryside as once the old lady's point-to-pointers had been driven over the jumps. Rowan, used to being driven too fast by her father, at least had never felt in his car that it might fly to bits at any minute, which made the journey with Millie a good deal more hair-raising. Rowan had to keep a hold on her hopes – she couldn't remember what Mrs Arbuthnot had said about her old circus horse . . . it was bound to be a crock, unacceptable to Lucy Prebble. She thought – too late – she should have got Matty on her side, telling her in advance of the plan. Sensing her anxiety, Auntie Millie patted her on the knee and said, 'You've a very nervous temperament, my child. It's bad for the horses.'

They found the Arbuthnot establishment after several false alarms – 'Yes, I remember, this is her lane. Her house is at the bottom' four times before the right house appeared. ('My memory is not what it was.') The lane was the worst yet, and the house a dilapidated bungalow set before an equally dilapidated stable yard – once a beautiful brick-built set of barns but now reinforced with breeze blocks and corrugated iron in necessary places, giving the whole place a decidedly one-eyed look.

'Poor old Amelia,' said Auntie Millie. 'She's not been the same since Archie died.'

Amelia Arbuthnot turned out to be another Auntie Millie as far as Rowan could see, the same weatherbeaten look and hip-unhappy walk, but she greeted them warmly. She largely ignored Rowan, and Rowan could see that there was to be a lot of reminiscing and irrelevant talk before they got down to business. She had to reconcile herself as they sat down in the untidy kitchen while Amelia set out ham and baked potatoes and packet bread. At any other time she would have found the horsy conversation interesting, but she was too sweaty with anticipation now to appreciate it. It seemed an age before the talk got around to the purpose of the visit.

Auntie Millie gave a graphic account of Lucy Prebble's tunnel vision and poor Matty's disability, and of how Rowan so desperately wanted to buy Birdie.

'You're the gel that rang me up?' Mrs Arbuthnot at last noticed that Rowan was there.

'Yes. You said you had an Andalusian circus horse that needed a good home. The Prebbles would be a terribly good home.'

'Hm.'

'I thought it would be worth having a look at him,' Auntie Millie said.

At last they got up from the table. The two old girls were talking about somebody called the Galloping Golightly as they tottered out into the stable yard and stood for another five minutes outside the barn door remembering a hunt with the Beaufort which had ended in disaster – hilarious by their squawks of laughter – then at last Amelia opened the door and they went inside.

There was a row of six loose-boxes, two of which were occupied.

'The end one,' said Amelia.

Rowan ran forward and peered over the door.

Somehow, because it was a circus horse, in spite of being told it was a bay, she had still expected spots or stripes or something ridiculous. But the horse was a bay, not commanding, but with a presence of great dignity and kindness. Looking at him, Rowan could sense it. He had large gentle eyes which surveyed her with the same curiosity as she bent on him. A beautiful head, a crested neck with a long mane, and a strong compact body. Clean black legs.

'Oh, he's beautiful!'

Auntie Millie snorted up behind her.

'Hmm.' After a long consideration, she said, 'Nice.'

'I can assure you,' Amelia said, 'as far as anything in this world is a certainty, this horse is safe, kind and honest. He would not harm a hair of your little girl's head.'

'Does he go on? She's no legs to use, remember.'

'Yes. He walks out. He obeys the word. If you want to trot you just say so.'

Rowan thought this was a frightfully good idea. Why weren't all horses trained like that?

‘What’s wrong with him?’

‘He’s getting on. He’s fifteen. His tendons wouldn’t stand a day’s hunting and jumping wouldn’t be wise. But hacking around – fine.’

‘It would get her going,’ Auntie Millie said.

‘Do you want to try him?’

‘Why not?’ said Auntie Millie.

Rowan had never thought to see Auntie Millie ride. Amelia fetched her a pair of steps from the tack-room and she climbed into the saddle and rode out into the paddock. The horse went with his neck arched, delicately mouthing his bit, and the old lady sat perfectly in the saddle, smiling. When she said ‘Trot’, the horse trotted, smooth as silk, and Auntie Millie sat without rising, like one piece with the horse. Rowan watched, entranced. The funny old bundle of clothes in the saddle rode like Charlie, like Josephine. When she cantered, she was as graceful as a girl, all in one with the perfectly collected horse.

When she came back to the gate, she said, ‘I don’t know about Matty, but I’ll take this horse off your hands, Amelia.’

‘Done,’ said Amelia.

‘How much are you asking?’

‘A gift to you, my dear. He needs a home.’

‘Great.’

'You can borrow my trailer and take him with you. You've got the Land-Rover, I see. I don't need the trailer for a month or so.'

'Why not?' said Auntie Millie.

The two old ladies set about connecting the Land-Rover to a decrepit trailer that was parked in a barn, while Rowan was told to untack the horse. She did so, bemused. She was wondering if her plan had gone haywire – it hadn't been her idea for Auntie Millie to have the horse, for goodness' sake! But the fact they were taking it back with them . . . she didn't know what to think. It was hopeless to ask. She might have been invisible for all the notice they took of her. They put straw in the trailer and a hay-net, and Amelia led the bay horse inside while Auntie Millie put up the back ramp. Then they kissed affectionately and Auntie Millie got into the driving seat.

'Oh, by the way, Rowan said he lies down for mounting. That could be very useful out in the country.'

'He stretches down, straddles his legs out and his back goes down about four inches. Just tap him behind the knees with your whip and say "Down".'

'Brilliant!'

Rowan hopped up. Auntie Millie started the

engine. Rowan shouted at Amelia, 'What's his name?'

'Matador,' she shouted back.

Matador for Matty, Rowan registered. But was he?

'Are you going to keep him?' she asked after they had bumped down the long drive and were out on the road.

Auntie Millie brayed with laughter.

'Poor Rowan! You've done a great job, dear, finding a horse like that. Now you're frightened I'm going to keep him! Well, I certainly will if Lucy Prebble is stupid enough to turn him down. We'll say he's *ours* just for now, see how it goes. You must have found out by now that you can't tell Lucy Prebble what's good for her. She has to be tricked.'

'How do you mean?'

'She has to make up her own mind. If you tell her, she'll jib. If she was a horse, she'd have been shot by now.'

Rowan wasn't sure what to make of this. Her plan had gone swimmingly but now seemed out of her control.

'Work on Matty,' Auntie Millie said.

Rowan was no wiser when they got home. It

transpired that Auntie Millie had no stable to put the horse in, and Rowan hadn't the nerve to take him to the Haweses. Perhaps Babar would have him – then she remembered.

'We've got a loose-box at home! We can put him there tonight.'

'Good thinking!'

In the now fading light they coasted down the long hill into the village and Auntie Millie pulled up outside the gate into Rowan's back garden. The lights were on in the cottage and there was a faint smell of baking on the air. Rowan had already cleaned out the loose-box and scrubbed the old manger; the roof was sound and the doors oiled.

'We'll unload him and put him in, then I'll go and fetch some hay and straw from Mr Bailey down the road.'

Rowan's mother, hearing their voices, came out to see what was going on.

'I'm borrowing your loose-box for a night or two, my dear, for a horse I've acquired. I'm sure you don't mind?'

Without waiting for an answer she bobbed back to the Land-Rover and drove away, leaving Pauline Watkins peering suspiciously over the half-door.

'Just tell me what you're up to, my girl!'

It had been a long day, and Rowan was no longer sure herself. She felt exhausted with all her conflicting emotions.

She said, 'It's that horse in Norfolk I told you about. Mrs Mildmay took me to look and liked him. He's hers now. That woman gave him to her.'

'I thought he was for Matty.'

Rowan didn't know any longer. She realized she felt very tired, shattered by the long, bone-shaking drive and the eternal doubts. Auntie Millie came back with feed and bedding and they made the horse comfortable and gave him a tin bath full of water. He seemed quite unfazed by his new quarters and fell to munching his hay. Rowan supposed his circus life had made him used to new quarters all the time.

'You can look after him for a few days,' Auntie Millie said when they were finished. 'Ride him out and let everyone see him. Tell them he belongs to me and you're keeping him for me until I get my stable mended. Let the gossip flow, my dear. You'll find Lucy Prebble will be along in no time.'

'But will you – do you want him – for your own?'

'Oh my dear, if only—! But those days are gone, I'm afraid. He's for Matty, like you said.'

At last, Rowan thought – she could sleep

happily! Her plan was working out. Auntie Millie was a darling. Her mother was looking confused, as well she might, but Auntie Millie gave her a quick hug and said, 'You've got a very determined daughter, my dear. You should be proud of her.'

She drove away.

'Should I?' asked Pauline Watkins dubiously.

But Rowan had no answer.

Rowan had a lesson the next evening after school with Josephine. When she went up to High Hawes she collected Birdie's saddle and bridle and, instead of catching her out of the field, she whizzed home on her bicycle and tacked up Matador. She had to let out the bridle which was a muddle and the bit was rather small and the saddle girth only met up with a colossal amount of tugging but eventually, flushed and anxious, she led Matador out of his stable into the lane and mounted him. She was trembling with anxiety. He felt enormous after Birdie but, somehow, kindness seemed to exude from him. She turned his head up the hill and he strode out happily, mouthing his bit, as light on her hand as Birdie and every bit as lovely.

By the time she turned into the yard at High Hawes she was alight with excitement. Nobody – but nobody – could fault this horse!

'What on earth—?'

First to see her was Lizzie. She let out a shriek. Hugh looked out of Cascade's box. His eyes came out on stalks.

'Whatever's that?'

Charlie came out of the feed shed with a hay-net over his shoulder, stopped in his tracks and said, 'Birdie's grown in the night! Whatever have you got there?'

'I've come for my lesson.'

'On what, might I enquire?'

'Matador.'

'And where did Matador come from?'

'He's Mrs Mildmay's.'

They positively reeled in their tracks.

'*Auntie Millie's?*'

'She put him in my loose-box till she's mended her own and she told me to exercise him. So I am.'

She touched Matador with her heels and he walked on to the gate of the school. The Haweses stood in a row and watched, speechless. Charlie opened it for her. She went through and started walking round, feeling herself flushing up as Charlie, Lizzie, Hugh and Shrimp leaned over the rails to watch. After two circuits, when no-one had said anything, she said softly, 'Trot', and Matador trotted. He tucked in his nose and went into a perfect dressage medium trot, as if she were a brilliant rider. But she only had to sit there. He felt as if he moved on springs, and to sit to his trot was as easy as sitting to his walk. And when he cantered it was like sitting in an armchair, gently floating round the school, riding on a cloud. She circled to the left and to the right, and came back to the gate to halt. He stood foursquare, like a statue.

Josephine had joined the silent row of spectators. They all stared, and Rowan smiled. She leaned forward and patted Matador's neck.

'Nice, isn't he?'

Charlie smiled. 'He's for Matty?'

They all started to scream at her, 'Where did you get him?' 'Did you buy him?' 'Is he really Auntie Millie's?' 'How did you find out about him?'

Charlie said, 'You are a clever little twit, Rowan, aren't you?' But he was still smiling. 'I think you might have got it right this time.'

Josephine wanted to try him, so did all the others. But Josephine said only her, and mounted him and Rowan watched this dream horse drifting round the school. With every stride he took her pride and happiness expanded, until she thought she would burst. The others were all leaping about shouting, 'Fantastic!' and 'Brill!' and 'Magic!'

Rowan tried to remember the drawbacks. 'He's fifteen and his tendons aren't very good. Light hacking only, she said.'

'He's perfect, Rowan.' Josephine brought him back to the gate. Charlie gave him a Polo mint out of his pocket and the horse bent his head and lifted it delicately between his lips. 'You're a great fellow.' Charlie patted his neck.

'What's the plan?'

'Gossip, Auntie Millie said. Mrs Prebble will hear the gossip and come and look.'

'Of course she will! Everyone who hears that Auntie Millie has got herself a horse will want to have a look.'

'If Mrs Mildmay is in charge, you can't go wrong,' Josephine said.

'You are clever, Rowan,' Lizzie breathed. 'We couldn't work out what you were up to, going home with Auntie Millie.'

'I said it was a plot,' Hugh shouted. 'I was right!'

Charlie laughed. 'Is she paying you livery, Rowan?'

Rowan was flooded with relief, that all her beloved Haweses were so approving. Josephine said she should forgo the lesson, and just hack out with Lizzie to give the horse an easy exercise before it got dark. So Rowan and Lizzie rode across the dusking downs and Rowan, at last, thought everything might turn out all right.

Rowan loved having a horse in her own loose-box. Going down in the morning, pulling on her anorak and smelling the first hint of autumn, seeing the last star fading over the top of the downs above as she went down the garden and hearing Matador's soft whicker of welcome as he heard her step, made getting up quite different. No snuggling back under the blankets when the alarm clock went off. If she was extra early she had time to take him out to graze on what was supposed to be their lawn for ten minutes after he had had his feed. And every evening she rode him out with Lizzie. Coming home, putting his bed right and filling his hay-net, she loved to lean over the door before she went in to watch him eating, clean and snug in the old box. Birdie might miss her, but Rowan was no longer anxious. She had done all that was possible to do and perhaps, if it all went wrong, she would still have Matador. It was too soon to count her chickens and Rowan had – at last – learned to be philosophical.

The gossip travelled. Jerry Patterson rang up to find out if he was hearing things – Auntie Millie had bought a horse???! Otty rang up, and Babar came round to see and have a ride. 'Oh, what a dream!'

Four nights later Matty came down. She was on her own, having swung all the way on her crutches. Rowan was in the stable, mucking out.

'I had to see this! Auntie Millie buying a horse! Why is he with you?'

'Just until her stable's mended,' Rowan said, trying to sound nonchalant.

'But she's all crocked up. She can't ride any more.'

'She thought he was suitable. That's the point.'

'Holy Cow, Auntie Millie riding!'

Matty laid her arms on the loose-box door and peered in. Matador turned round and came to see if there were any Polo mints.

'Well, you're a nice man, I must say.' Matty laughed. 'Someone said he was a circus horse. I thought he'd be one of those spotted wonders.'

'He's brilliant. You just have to say, and he does it.'

'Like what?'

'Look.'

Rowan sent up a prayer. She touched Matador behind the knees with the broom handle and said, 'Down.'

Matador turned his head and looked at her, as if in surprise. He scraped his hind legs out behind him like a dog stretching, and slid his forelegs out in front of him and went down so that his belly was not far off floor level. Rowan slipped on to his back, and Matador slithered his feet back underneath him. Then he turned to Matty for another titbit.

Matty was impressed. 'That's great. It's all right getting on with a chair in the stable yard, but not much good if you have to get off in the country and there's not a gate or a bank for miles. Great for Auntie Millie.'

'That's what she said. But I don't know if she's going to keep him. A friend gave him to her. She told me she didn't really think she could ride again, but he was too lovely to refuse.'

'Might you have him?'

'I don't know. He's fantastic to ride.'

Matty opened the loose-box door. 'Tell him to go down again.'

Rowan gave the aids, and Matador straddled himself out again. Matty hopped forward and was on his back in one quick movement. Matador gathered himself up again and turned back to his hay-net, snatching a mouthful.

'Hey, that's great!' Matty laughed.

Her head was nearly touching the rafters. She said, 'Go and get his bridle and I'll ride him out.'

Rowan fetched the bridle, feeling really scared. She knew she shouldn't do it, but she also knew she must. She put the bridle on and passed the reins back to Matty.

'It feels fantastic!'

Matty was as white as a sheet, and more scared than Rowan.

'You only have to tell him,' said Rowan. 'Walk.'

'Open the door.'

Rowan opened it. Matty said, 'Walk on,' and rode out into the garden. The gate into the lane was open where Rowan had come in on her bike, and Matty rode out of the gate and turned up the lane. She was bareback and had no hat on. Rowan ran after her.

'I say, Matty!'

But Matty didn't stop or even turn round. Matador was walking out with his eager springy pace, disappearing up the lane in the beginning of the evening dusk. Rowan watched her, feeling sick with responsibility – was it all her fault, or a bit Matty's? All hers, she suspected.

She supposed she ought to go with her. But then she assumed Matty would be back in a minute. She finished off the mucking out, only a matter of a couple of minutes and then, worried, went to look up the lane. But there was no sign of Matty coming back. Rowan went and fetched her bike. 'She's gone to call on the Haweses,' she thought. It was obvious – see their faces!

Excited, Rowan pedalled up the hill, head down. It was just starting to go dusk and the sort of evening that smelled amazing and promised all sorts of exciting things ahead. Or so Rowan always thought. She was half laughing, half frightened, at the success of her plan. Matty riding into the yard at High Hawes . . . they would all die, seeing her! Rowan couldn't wait.

She pedalled into the yard, but it was all quiet. She went round the back, and found only Shrimp bringing Bonzo in from the field.

'Hi! Have you seen her?'

'Seen who?' asked Shrimp.

'Matty. Matty riding!'

'Matty riding? Never! Who on – you mean—?'

'Isn't she here?'

'I haven't seen her.'

'What about the others?'

'They're having tea. Matty hasn't been here. Nobody's seen her that I know of.'

'But she came up here, riding Matador.'

'She must have gone past.'

'Did you hear her? Did you hear hooves on the road?'

'Now you come to think of it, yes. Bonzo whinnied. I thought it was you. About five minutes ago.'

'Where's she gone?'

Rowan, thinking of Matty bareback, hatless . . . what was she thinking of, to have ridden away? Matty all alone, not even her crutch . . . the plan was working so well it was terrifying.

'She must have gone on the downs,' Shrimp said. 'Where else?'

'Oh, I don't believe it!'

There was no denying her flooding guilt now. Was Matty mad? Rowan ran towards the house and the rock that was Joan Hawes. She would know what to do. They were all sitting round the table eating and were startled by her hysterical arrival. 'Matty's gone!' she wailed.

Hugh thought it was terribly funny – 'What you wanted, wasn't it?' – Charlie and Josephine looked serious and Joan Hawes said, 'But it's nearly dark! Are you sure she's gone on the downs?'

'Where else could she go? She didn't come back.'

'It's the most likely place,' Charlie said.

'She's got no saddle!'

'But if that horse is the magic horse he appears to be, no harm will come to her,' Josephine said sensibly.

'It's strange ground to him,' Charlie said.

'And it's dark. The child is mad,' Joan Hawes said abruptly. 'Really – you children! We'll have to go and look for her.'

'Josephine and I can ride up – we'll find her,' Charlie said. 'Don't worry. She won't have gone far.'

'I don't want Lucy Prebble up here, for goodness' sake! Demanding to know where she is. Off you go, and hurry up. Rowan, you are a lunatic.'

'I thought she was just going up a bit and back! I didn't know she'd just go!'

'You stay with me. We'll go in the Land-Rover. Lizzie and Hugh, you stay here. You can deal with Mrs Prebble if she rings up. Or no, on second thoughts, don't answer the phone. We want Matty back first – if we're lucky, Lucy won't find out.'

They scattered. As Rowan ran out, Josephine caught her arm and whispered, 'Cheer up, Rowan, he won't hurt her. Remember, the girl's a great rider.'

And Rowan, running for the Land-Rover, held on to that thought.

* * *

Matty, coming out through the trees, saw a new moon, a thin sliver of light, shivering over the shoulder of the far down. She knew that you wished on a new moon. The wish was easy: 'I want – oh, I *want* – to do all this again, to be *able*— To ride. To run. Not to be hopping like a frog.' The horse's soft coat, just darkening with winter, was warm under her thighs and the intelligent ears were pricked up ahead, watching the chalky path in the dusk. Matty turned him on to the grass. She knew this way so well. It was like coming home, passing the sarsen stone, turning uphill where the way divided, following the footprints where the Haweses exercised. The horse strode out, kind and willing.

She had only meant, after all, to go up the lane and back. But Matty had forgotten that now, revelling in the excitement that flooded her. She hadn't even thought that she wanted to ride again – not all that aggro with her mother again! But this was something else, this feeling of total trust in the horse moving quietly up towards the stars that glittered over the black crest of the down. Matty felt she could touch them. When she gained the summit she could see in every direction, across the dark horizons of the downs beyond and back to the lights of the village in the valley directly below. She felt like God.

She only had to say to him, 'Trot', and then 'Canter', and then she was floating along between the earth and the sky, the muffled thud of hooves the only sound, the cold air flying past her cheeks, the long mane streaming out between her hands. Everything had come right at last and she knew she could ride for ever.

When Matty didn't come home and it was dark, Mrs Prebble rang the Haweses. Lizzie and Hugh heard the phone ringing but, acting on instructions, didn't answer it. Mrs Prebble then rang Pauline Watkins.

'Is Matty with you?'

'Not that I know of. Rowan's out in the stable. I'll go and ask her.'

Pauline Watkins went down the garden to find an empty stable, no sign of either Rowan or Matty, and a pair of crutches lying in the grass. 'Don't panic,' she said to herself. She wasn't sure what she was most frightened of: what Rowan and Matty were getting up to, or what Mrs Prebble was going to say about it.

'Gone out on a *horse*?' bawled Lucy Prebble. 'What horse?'

'It belongs to Mrs Mildmay.'

'*Mrs Mildmay!* What sort of a horse?'

'Don't ask me. Big and brown. You'd better ask her yourself.'

'I most certainly will! I shall be over directly.'

Pauline Watkins groaned. She had no idea, when it all got technical. Was Rowan to blame? It was part of the ploy to get Mrs Prebble to let them have Birdie, she remembered, but Mrs Prebble had sounded far from happy. The more she thought about her, the less Pauline Watkins wanted to face Mrs Prebble. After a few minutes' thought, she got out her car and drove up to High Hawes. She had thought to find it buzzing, but when she drove into the yard everything was silent and in darkness. She turned off her engine and sat there, feeling annoyed.

Lizzie and Hugh, hiding in the feed-shed, realized who it was and came out reluctantly. They told her what had happened.

Then Mrs Prebble arrived.

Then Auntie Millie.

Then Joan Hawes and Rowan.

They all stood talking nineteen to the dozen in the stable yard. Rowan crept out with Lizzie. They ran out through the wood and to the gate that led out on to the downs. Rowan was in tears again, and Lizzie white-faced.

'They're going to ring the police!'

'Auntie Millie won't let them,' Lizzie said stoutly. 'Don't be stupid. If she's out there, it's because she's enjoying it. Isn't that what you wanted?'

'Yes!'

'Well then. Charlie and Josephine will bring her back, don't worry. There's nothing wrong.'

'Yet! Mrs Prebble's furious!'

'She's always like that – you know that. Mum will cool her down. And Auntie Millie will shut her up. And everything will be all right.'

'Suppose—'

'Oh, shut up! She'll be all right!'

They leaned on the gate looking up at the dark crest of the downs. The new moon hung there, bright and consoling.

'Have you ever ridden in the dark?' Lizzie asked. 'It's lovely.'

'Like the night you rode Birdie at camp? It was like this, wasn't it?'

'Yes. And it turned out all right. So will this.'

Rowan was shivering. They neither of them wanted to go back.

'Auntie Millie will have sorted it all out now.

They'll be boozing in the kitchen. They'll be buttering up Mrs Prebble.'

'I hope so.'

They sat on the gate, waiting. After what seemed a very long time, they thought they heard the sound of voices, the chink of a hoof on the chalk.

'Listen!'

Somebody laughed.

'It's Matty,' Lizzie whispered.

They opened the gate, and in the darkness saw the gleam of moonlight on three dark horses moving slowly down the hill towards them. Charlie was in front on Out of the West, Matty next, and Josephine bringing up the rear on Wilfred.

'It's us!' Lizzie shouted. 'Everyone's waiting for you!'

'Who's everyone?' Charlie asked.

They pulled up and heard the story. 'All of them, all waiting,' Lizzie said. 'We couldn't bear it.'

'No harm's done,' said Charlie.

Matty, riding past, leaned down to Rowan and said, 'He's wonderful.'

They rode on and Lizzie and Rowan followed. When they got to the yard Rowan went up to Matty and said, 'I'll take him home.'

'You can put him in a box and come indoors,'

Charlie said. 'If everyone's there, you should—'

'No! I'll take him.'

Before he could say any more she snatched the reins out of Matty's hands and led him away out of the yard. He came kindly. Rowan walked on dumbly down the long hill to home, seeing their long shadows bobbing across the lane. The horse had looked after her. Matty's eyes had been shining under the dark swing of her black hair. She was like a new person.

'Dear Matador,' Rowan said.

His hay-net was hanging up and the bed forked out. Rowan slipped off his bridle and shut the door behind him. She stayed there, watching him. It was cold now, with the smell of autumn and the dew heavy in the trampled grass, the smell of cows coming up from the river. If she went to the gate she could hear the soft cropping of the ponies on the far bank, see the white ghost of Cascade and the shadow that was Birdie. *Her* Birdie. When would her mother come?

But it was Charlie who came.

He found her sitting outside the stable door, her head buried in her arms.

'They're all celebrating up there,' he said. 'Laughing and shouting. Why don't you come?'

'Is it all right?'

'Yes, she's like a cat purring. She's given you Birdie. She wants to see you. I think she wants to give you a kiss.'

He laughed.

'You're joking!'

'No, truly. Would I, about you and Birdie?'

'You mean, it's all right?'

'I've told you, it's all right.'

And Rowan burst into tears again, and went back to High Hawes with Charlie.

THE END

THE SWALLOW TALE
K.M. PEYTON

Rowan made no effort to get up – it was so awful. Swallow . . . her darling Swallow! Nearly killing her . . .

From the moment she first sees him, Rowan is head over heels in love with Swallow, the reckless, spirited bay pony, who enters her life with a bang – literally. But wild Swallow is hard to handle, especially for an inexperienced rider like Rowan. As she struggles to master him, Rowan suffers falls, bruises and plenty of teasing. Is Swallow really worth the agony? It takes a suspicious-looking man to turn up, claiming Swallow as his own, to make Rowan realize she'd go through it all over again – if she can only keep her beloved pony . . .

THE FIRST TITLE IN THE HIGH HORSE SERIES

'Give K.M. Peyton a stable and a collection of fallible characters and she will return you a compulsively readable story'
The Times

0 552 528072

THE SWALLOW SUMMER
K.M. PEYTON

'Loose horse! Loose horse!'
'It's Swallow!' shrieked Shrimp . . .

Summer has come to High Hawes, which means the annual Pony Club camp – and Rowan is terrified. She still hasn't managed to master wild Swallow, the spirited bay pony with a will of his own, and she's bound to humiliate herself in front of the brilliant Hawes family. But once at camp, even worse is to come when the future of the Hawes' riding school – including Swallow – is threatened. To Rowan's horror, she realizes that her darling pony may now have to be sold . . .

THE SECOND TITLE IN THE HIGH HORSE SERIES

0 552 529699